"A Heaviness That's Gone

"Let us not burden our remembrance with a heaviness that's gone."

- *The Tempest, Act 5 Scene 1*

There are some memories which are so visceral, so tangible, that they hardly count as memories at all. Memories are supposed to be in the past. Something you can move on from. But there are some memories which only grow more painful as time passes, because it reminds you of just how stuck in the past they are.

It forces you to realise they're gone.

When I think of those days, I realise just how conflicted I still am about what happened. On one hand, I would give anything to go back and relive every moment properly, instead of just laying in the dark, trying to remember the sound of her laugh, the smell of the fire, the warmth of his smile. On the other hand, however, nothing in the world could convince me to have to live through that again.

I'm thankful I have no choice.

CHAPTER ONE

"To set a gloss on faint deeds, hollow welcomes,

Recanting goodness, sorry ere 'tis shown;

But where there is true friendship, there needs none"

- *Timon of Athens*

The first time I saw Northam Manor, it was practically buried under two foot of snow. I remember trying to carry my boxes up the stone stairs, having to pause every few seconds to push the windswept hair out of my eyes. My parents had barely stopped the car to let me out, driving away with a quick "see you in the summer" before the tyres screeched and they were gone, leaving me staring up at the old stone building with all the nerves of a student transferring mid term. I won't get into why I transferred - it's boring, long-winded, and has no relevance to the wider story. It's at Northam that the true story takes place.

It is so strange to think back to that day. So much was going to change in such a short period of time. I had no idea what was waiting for me up those stairs, and I can't help but wonder if I would have still climbed up them if I had known. If I'd known about all the adventures, all the magic, all the excitement, I would have ran up them, no doubt. But if I'd known the full story, would I have chased after my parents? I don't think I would have. Even now, knowing what I do, I still think it was worth it.

I met Louis on my fourth trip up the stairs that first morning; he was perched on the banister watching as I struggled with the cases.

"Stop!" he ordered, jumping down and scanning me from behind his glasses. I raised an eyebrow, taking in the taller boy in front of me. I don't actually remember if he was holding a camera, but I can say with practical certainty that he was. It was less of an accessory and more an extra limb, never without it.

"Your coat, it's covered in snowflakes. It's beautiful. Do you mind?" he asked, motioning towards his camera. I couldn't think of an appropriate response so I just nodded, letting him lean in and photograph the side of my shoulder. I couldn't see anything remarkable, just snowflakes on dark green wool. It looked normal. Boring, even. But that was a common theme with Louis. He could make even the most mundane sight in the world look magical.

As a history student, we learn to analyse sources. In the first lesson, we are taught to write down everything we can possibly see, no matter how seemingly trivial. I had a professor once who, when I complained about this, told me that it was the simple things we often forget first. This struck a chord with me, and over time I've come to realise the first thing I do upon meeting new people is create a mental list of my initial observations.

Even now, when I think about Louis, I see him the same way I did that first winter. Lanky, pale, serious. Curls falling across his forehead, his glasses steamed up. Woolen sleeves pulled over his hands.

Full of life.

After that initial first conversation, I spent most the day unpacking in my room. It hit me just how impersonal the space was; apart from a few history textbooks and my jacket over the chair, it was practically unchanged from when I first opened the door. I didn't have any photos or memorabilia; nothing showing any hint of a personality at all. That would come to change over the next year - Northam really did help me grow as a person.

I met Alec and Soph at the same time, when I finally mustered the courage to venture into the shared kitchen. I found them in a position I would soon realise was commonplace. Whenever I think of them, that is how I imagine them; Alec stood on the sofa, Soph laying on the floor. It was as though one was trying to make himself as big as possible, the other as small. Over time I would realise this was perfectly representative of the two, but on that first day all I could do was watch and stare.

"Hence! home, you idle creatures get you home!" Alec shouted, flinging his arm out as he looked into the distance in a dramatic fashion.

The girl stared up at him, hesitating before quietly replying with "home before us. Fair and noble hostess, we are your guest to-night".

I frowned, recognising the quote but not having time to place it before Alec called out "night, thou sober-suited matron, all in black!".

Before Soph could respond, Alec noticed me, bounding over to me, gripping my shoulders and giving me his signature grin.

"You must be room five! About bloody time too! What's your name? Have you unpacked?"

I stammered against the sudden questions, gaping at him before muttering my name.

"Sebastian! Like from Twelfth Night! I'm Alec," he replied, stressing the C sound. "And this is Soph. Put your stuff down! What are you studying?"

Over time I came to realise that Alec spoke exclusively with exclamation marks. If one was to transcribe Alec's speech, it would be in capital letters. He lived his life out loud.

These Shakespeare contests were commonplace within our group, and looking back, I believe over half of what Soph said aloud were quotes from famous authors, as though she was scared of original thought. Everyone would join in when they could, and even with my limited knowledge of literature I could give it a go. It always came down to Soph and Alec in the end though, but that was hardly surprising. How could anyone possibly compete with theatre and classical literature students in a Shakespeare contest?

I can't deny I was a tiny bit intimidated by Alec to start with; there was something scary about someone who was so honest, so truthful, so confident. That first week I'd grown to know the three of them, and whilst Sophie and Louis seemed content to simply offer quiet conversation until I opened up, Alec had much more of a blunt and direct approach. That's not to say I didn't grow to love Alec just as I did them all, but merely it took me a little longer to become used to him.

Our group wasn't completed for another week, when I finally saw Kitty. I'd already been told by Louis that I shouldn't expect to see a lot of her during the weekend, as she was often holed up in her studio.

In the end, I saw perhaps too much of her.

In my defense, the doors all looked the same along the corridor. It was only a matter of time before I pushed against the fourth door and not the fifth. It just so happened that this time, when it happened, I was met with two girls, half-dressed. I yelled out an apology and turned away in panic, flooded with relief when I merely heard a delighted laugh. This will forever be the noise I associate with Kitty. I don't remember turning around again, but somehow I was very suddenly face to face with a tiny girl, jet black hair bouncing in curls across her bare shoulders. I don't quite remember how much paint was smudged on her face and hair, but knowing Kitty it was almost a certainty.

"You're...Sebastian, right? Room 5?"

I nodded, desperately trying to avoid the other girl dressing in the corner. I blushed at the sight of her tattoos - roses, beginning at the bottom of her spine and winding right up her side. I quickly averted my eyes, turning my attention back to the girl in front of me.

"Uh...yeah. Call me Seb. You must be, um...Katherine?"

The girl from the corner laughed again, finally pulling on a shirt and joining us in the doorway.

"She'll kill you in your sleep if you call her Katherine. This is Kitty, I'm Daniela. I don't technically live here, but Kit has a larger bed than I, so.." She trailed off suggestively, grinning again before kissing Kitty on the cheek and slipping out of the room.

Daniela was never technically in our group, given that she lived across campus and belonged to a different school department, and yet she was just as much of our mismatched family as the rest of us. She wasn't here as regularly, but she was there for every event that year, and once something like that happens, there's no coming back. She was the steadiest of the group, always there with an easy smile and flawless eyeliner. Logically I should have been intimidated by her, but she had that natural quality that made me instantly love her, and that never wavered.

"-Anyways, as Dani said, I'm Kitty. You're studying history, right? Any art history on your syllabus?"

One thing that was always consistent with Kitty was that she could get art into any conversation. She was flawlessly beautiful in a way that made it look effortless; messy buns and paint smudges. By this point - only a week into term - I hadn't actually seen any of her artwork, but over the years I would become more familiar with her artistic style than with my own home. That was the magic in creation, I found. I could recognise Kitty's brushstrokes and Louis' photos, no matter what. I could still close my eyes and hear Alec's performances, his voice projecting across the stage. And Soph's words would forever hold their own quality that was so remarkably individual. The most consistent part of my time at Northam was that I always longed to have something like their art - something I could put out into the world. Maybe that's why I'm writing this.

After those first introductions, the group was set in stone. I suppose that's what happens when you put five people in such close confines. For those outside the group, we were probably just seen as isolated, elitist even. We were all well aware of the looks we got, parading around in trench coats, quoting shakespeare and referencing classic literature. People were always obsessed with staring at the 'Northamers', as we came to be known. It was a mix of jealousy and mystery, I think. The jealousy disappeared, of course, afterwards.

I would have taken jealousy over pity any day of the week.

Anyway, pity was unavoidable, all things considered.

To those living in Northam, however, the mystery disappeared. It's like source analysis; someone can study a source from the outside with all the knowledge in the world, but there will always be something you miss unless you're at the heart of it. This was just the same. Take Kitty, for example. To everyone outside, she was merely seen as a stunning beauty. They saw her holding hands with Dani, saw her laughing loudly as she walked along walls, arms thrown out for balance. For me, though, she was the truest when she was curled up in the armchair we dragged into the kitchen, bleary eyed. It always took her at least an hour and three cups of coffee to properly wake up, so it wasn't unusual to find her in the kitchen in her pyjamas. There was no way the outside world could know that Alec got migraines, that Soph loved silent movies, that Dani let Kitty colour in her tattoos when she was stressed.

The most open of us all was Louis. His camera allowed him to have conversations with the most random of people - I once found him crouched on the floor outside the science lab, talking with the cleaner about her shoes. There was an endearing quality about him that made everyone think they knew him, even after only five minutes. Yet even he appeared different inside than out. It's impossible for me to pinpoint exactly how he was different, but there was just a quality about him that was inherently private. When I saw him curled up on his bed (his door was always open, no matter what), his curls obscuring his eyes, or when I heard him swear softly under his breath as he burned his toast for the fifth time that day, I couldn't help but smile to myself. Us six were the only people who saw each other like that, and that was an honour. Despite everything; despite all the heartbreak, despair and trauma which I would come to associate with Northam, it was the sleepy, silent mornings which would forever mean home to me.

It's important to note that not all my time at school was spent in Northam. After all, I was the only one of us studying history, and so it was inevitable that I would make other friends. There was the dark haired girl who sat next to me in my European Renaissance class, and a guy who shared notes about The Cold War with me. I was friendly with them, but I don't even remember their names. Whilst I was there to study history, it paled in comparison to the time spent with the group. I was more than grateful for the course, but ultimately Northam - not the school - was what changed me that year.

CHAPTER TWO

"As in a theatre, the eyes of men,

After a well-grac'd actor leaves the stage,

Are idly bent on him that enters next,

Thinking his prattle to be tedious."

- *Richard II*

Some of the best evenings I had at Northam were at Alec's performances. I was privy to so many of the rehearsals, the panicked evenings spent with Soph calmly running lines with him as he tore his hair out, that I was probably as word perfect as the actors, and yet as I approached the theatre I still felt a thrill of excitement. There was something so exhilarating about live theatre - as prepared as the actors were, there was always something that could go wrong. It was what made it exciting, dangerous even. Alec once said it gave him a huge rush, stepping on stage, and it was easy to see why.

"You know, this play had to be cancelled in theatres because of World War Two. They closed down all the theatres because of the Blitz, and so all productions had to be put on hold," I announced as we entered the foyer, laughing as Kitty rolled her eyes. She had a habit of doing that, especially when Dani wasn't around to monitor her.

"Uh oh everyone! We've reached the 'Seb bores us all with historical trivia' time of day." I flipped her off, nodding good-humouredly.

"Sure, sure. You all dig into me, and yet we all know Soph is just as interested in useless trivia as me, isn't that right?"

We all turned to look at her, waiting with raised eyebrows. She blushed, tucking her hair behind her ear before sighing.

"Fine! The title - Present Laughter - comes from Twelfth Night, from the quote "present mirth hath present laughter. And it only took Coward six days to write it. And -"

She was cut off by the ushers telling us to take our seats, which again made Kitty laugh. I loved the sight of her laugh - it went way past her mouth and instead enveloped her entire body. You could practically see her shining.

"Aw, don't worry Soph, I enjoyed your trivia," Louis murmured, squeezing her shoulder gently. He had such a quiet, subtle way with her, seemingly the only person she truly felt at ease with. At first I thought he had a crush on her - after all, she was beautiful, even if it was in less of an obvious way than Kitty - but when I mentioned this to Alec he laughed so hard he choked on his coffee. At the time I'd been confused, but over time I'd come to realise that his love for her was comparable to that of siblings. Even in appearances they seemed related, both with soft features and light brown curls. I remember the night in the theatre, watching them smile. There was something so beautiful about their smiles.

It's what I miss the most.

"And don't worry Seb, I love your trivia too," Louis added, grinning over Sophie's head. I rolled my eyes, trying to contain my smile. Back then, I was always worried about being too enthusiastic. They were my first proper group of friends, everything I did made me terrified I would lose them. I did everything I could to be a good friend; attended every showcase, made every cup of tea, made sure I was a shoulder to cry on. Looking back, I realise where I went wrong.

"So Seb," Louis muttered as the lights went down and the orchestra began to play. "Bet you anything Alec ends up shirtless at some point." I laughed in response, unable to reply as the play began.

Watching Alec perform was like watching a firework. It started with contained anticipation, where we were all sat in excitement. He started subtly, his words carrying across the stage and throughout the audience. It built and built, reaching a dramatic crescendo where he bursts into tears, the pure rage splintering as he all but yelled his lines. It was almost painful to watch, and yet it was still stunningly beautiful. The way the stage lights coated his features in red and blue and his eyeliner clung to his eyelashes is still vividly ingrained in my mind; the same way in which Kitty's laugh and Louis' smile feel real every time I think of them.

Alec was the star of the show, naturally, but it would be wrong to talk about the performance without addressing the sheer brilliance of all the other actors. I remember the actress playing Daphne being tragically beautiful, perfectly matched with the dark humour of Alec's Garry. I've always been in awe of actors; the ability to change who you are is a skill I've so often wished I had.

I have a copy of Present Laughter at the side of my bed even now, earmarked and damaged. I look through it on tough nights, nights where my hands won't stop shaking and my brain runs just a tad too quickly. There's one passage which I always come back to.

>   'There's something awfully sad about happiness, isn't there?'

That night, when I saw Alec performing his heart out on the stage, the quote just rushed past me and I barely took any notice. It made no sense to me; as I sat in the theatre surrounded by people who had very quickly become my family, with people I love more than anything, I couldn't imagine how anyone could be sad whilst also being happy. Looking back on it though, I realise what the quote meant. When you're happy, it truly makes you realise just how sad you were before. My life pre-Northam seems bleaker than I realised when living it, and now post-Northam seems even worse. I can no longer read that quote without remembering how stupidly unaware I was - I really didn't know just how happy I was.

I've said that quote countless times over the years, to countless people. It became somewhat of a mantra, something I would use to comfort myself whenever I needed it. I only ever said it to Louis once, though, despite me associating the quote most with him. It was in the kitchen, the night before…. Well, I guess I'll tell that story later.

Like the quote says: it's awfully sad.

For now, let's focus on happier things, like the look of pride on Kitty's face as she watched him perform. The thing you have to understand about Kitty is that no matter how snarky and confident she could seem, she truly, deeply loved her friends. She was watching him with her mouth slightly open, her eyes shining as she followed him in amazement. Soph once joked that Alec and Kitty were platonic soulmates, and in times like this it was clear to see where she was coming from. And yet, her pride wasn't limited to Alec; Kitty had unlimited love. It was easy to feel as though I was the exception to Kitty's rule, but I suppose that was unavoidable. She went to every one of Alec's plays, she bought every piece of Soph's published writing, and she got tickets to every gallery exhibition of Louis' photography. And then there was Daniela - I don't think I ever heard Kit listen to any music not composed by her girlfriend. It was inevitable that she would struggle to properly appreciate my work, given that it all rested on an essay; hardly the most exciting showcase of talent. But it never once bothered me. She had a special way of making even the littlest things seem valuable, even if it was simply a joke she laughed at a little too loud.

She lived her entire life to make people happy. She created art because she wanted to add more beauty to the world, and yet her entire existence added enough beauty for a lifetime.

But that's enough about Kitty. This was Alec's night, and even Kitty's limitless beauty couldn't outshine just how radiant he looked as he took his final bow. Over the years I saw Alec in so many roles; I saw his tortured Hamlet, his unhinged Macbeth, and nobody can forget his Atticus Finch from second year. But for me, this was the role of a lifetime for him. Garry Essendine: a flippant, humourous actor suffering from a mid-life crisis, struggling with what happiness truly means. For all of Alec's dramatic theatrics, deep down he suffered just as we all did. That much would certainly become apparent.

The night of the Present Laughter performance was also the night of my first Northam party. From what I remember (though I must admit, my memories of that night are somewhat hazy), the theme was 40s dress up, in honour of - as Alec put it - "Noel Coward, the Shakespeare of our century". At the time I didn't understand why so many people had attended the party; after all, we didn't know many people outside of our inner circle. I came to realise that people mostly just wanted to unearth the secrets of Northam - I have no doubt they were disappointed when they discovered nothing more magical than a threadbare sofa and a few chipped glasses. Even so, Dani had spent most of the evening draping fairy lights from the ceiling as Kitty offered what she called "artistic direction" from the sofa.

That was also the same night I realised the extremes my friends went to when it came to costumes. I remember how long I stood in front of my wardrobe, trying to find anything remotely 1940s themed. I would soon come to realise that no matter how long I stood there, I would never have matched the effort made by the others.

I still have a photo from that night on my bedside table, slightly faded but still perfectly visible. The remarkable thing about this photo was that, unusually, it wasn't taken by Louis. After all these years I've forgotten who actually took it; perhaps someone from the cast maybe, or even one of the girls who were constantly following Louis around back then. Either way, I'm grateful to whoever took it.

Kitty and Daniela were in the centre of the photo, arms wrapped around each other as they danced to some period-inappropriate song. (As a history student let me tell you, the anachronisms were headache inducing. I still remember Louis's laugh when I pointed this out.)

Anyway, the photograph.

Kitty and Daniela were trying to replicate the famous photograph from Times Square - the one with the sailor kissing the nurse. They'd clearly been mid-kiss when the photo was taken; Kitty's head thrown back as she laughed in Dani's arms. It made my heart hurt to see them both that happy. Off to one side was Alec, still dressed in his costume from the play, draped across the counter. His waistcoat was open and across his chest someone had written "Future Oscar Winner" in what looked like blood but was probably lipstick. Alec was always the first drunk and the last asleep at parties. Like I said - he lived out loud.

And then in the other corner stood me, Louis and Soph. I don't actually remember what we were discussing but based on the easy smile across all three faces, it was nothing too serious. I was speaking, gesturing wildly like I always did when I got excited. Soph was laughing gently, halfway through tucking her hair behind her ear, and Louis was watching me with an easy, soft smile on his face. That was one of the things I loved the most about him - he always gave me his full attention.

It's certainly not the only photograph with us all in, but it's one of the only candids. It acts as such a perfect vignette of life back then, which is why it hurts so much to look at. There's nothing staged, nobody is acting. It's real.

The party went on through the night, and I remember the evening in snippets.

Kitty, throwing her arms around me and screaming in my ear so loudly it hurt. Staggering out onto the landing with Louis, trying to find somewhere safe to hide his camera. Alec, stood on the table, performing the Hamlet monologue with a watermelon in place of the skull. Even Soph joined me for a dance, surprising even herself with her sudden gasp of laughter.

By the time the party finished, we had all resigned ourselves to a night spent in the garden. Not a single inch of our quarters wasn't covered with glass bottles, and after a night full of dancing we'd all piled onto the grass to cool down. I laid with Soph's head on my chest, hand tangled in her hair.

"Dine with my father, drink a health to me; For I must hence; and farewell to you all," Alec called out, raising the bottle of wine he was holding up high. I'd come to understand the rules of the Shakespeare game over my weeks there - essentially just say a quote which starts with the last word of the previous quote - and for once I was able to contribute.

"All the world's a stage, and all the men and women merely players," I added, and everyone froze. I briefly worried I had somehow misunderstood the game, before Dani burst into applause.

"Ladies and Gentlemen, please welcome Sebastian to the game! About bloody time," Kitty laughed, toasting me with whatever mixed concoction she was drinking out of an old mug. They all laughed, and I remember feeling an overwhelming sense of belonging. Even if it was with practically the most basic Shakespeare quote known to man, I'd still managed to play my part.

We eventually fell silent, once only Soph had been able to continue the game. As I slipped in and out of consciousness, I remember shivering against the cold breeze, regretting my decision to wear simply a white shirt with suspender braces. In the last moment before falling asleep, I heard a soft thud and felt something fall across my chest. In my exhausted state I didn't even think to question it, merely accepting the additional warmth and closing my eyes again.

Of course, at the time I didn't know, but just two foot away, Louis - now without his jacket - also closed his eyes.

CHAPTER THREE

"I have heard of your paintings too, well enough;

God has given you one face,

and you make yourselves another."

- *Hamlet*

I said earlier that I could have recognised Kitty's artwork no matter what. This wasn't always the case. It was a bit of a joke amongst us that I had an embarrassing lack of knowledge when it came to art; I'd developed a passable understanding of theatre and music from my friendship with Alec and Dani, and I could vaguely discuss the classics with Soph, but art was really not my speciality. This had become painfully apparent when we visited an exhibition about the pre-Raphaelites, and whilst everyone else was discussing Rossetti and Millais, I had merely been able to stammer out a wild guess about Van Gogh. It was a sign of just how much of a family we were that whilst they did laugh at me, it wasn't in a cruel way in the slightest. Even so, I was desperate to improve my knowledge of art in even the smallest way. For weeks, Kitty's artwork had been contained within her studio, and the only hints I'd seen were based on the smudges that permanently coated her hands and clothes.

When she'd asked me to bring her lunch to her studio, I'd been nervous. I remember fearing that I wouldn't be able to come up with an appropriate response; the art world seemed too distant, too isolated. Kitty always was beauty personified, and it seemed as though her artwork was too private a thing for me to properly comprehend. It turned out I didn't need to worry; the studio spoke for itself.

The first thing I noticed when I stepped inside was the overwhelming smell of oil paints. It almost made my eyes water, making me slightly lightheaded. I never did understand how Kitty lived with it.

The second thing was how at ease Kitty seemed, sat at the easel with a paintbrush tucked behind her ear. I hope I've already made clear just how confident Kitty was no matter where, always bouncy.

Full of life. But here, within her own room, she seemed truly at peace. It was as though all the energy had been taken away and she'd simply been left with a pure love for her work. She could just sit in the quiet, only the noise of Dani's music playing softly through her headphones.

Ironically, the last thing I'd noticed was the artwork itself. There were canvasses *everywhere*. It was hard to know what the walls and floor actually looked like, as it was completely covered in paint, paper and tarps. There was something so intrinsically Kitty about the entire room. It was chaotic, messy and beautiful. So, so beautiful.

"Hey Seb! Thanks, I really need to get this portrait fixed before my class tomorrow and just didn't have the time to head back over to get lunch. Did you find the room okay?"

I nodded, still staring up at the walls in amazement.

"Uh...yeah, no problem. Kit - these are, these are incredible." I knew she'd probably received hundreds of compliments eternally more intelligent and impressive than mine, but her face lit up regardless.

"Thank you! Hey, I reckon you'll like these ones. Here-" She pulled a large canvas out from behind her easel, brushing some dust off before handing it to me.

I recognised it immediately. It was clearly based on Liberty Leading The People, the only painting I knew anything about. My mind flooded with facts about the contextual history - 1830, revolutions in France, the eventual toppling of Charles X. But this was clearly Kitty's version of it - instead of the tricolour it was a pride flag, instead of faceless aristocrats it was people of all colours, shapes and sizes. The banners no longer read "Liberté, égalité, fraternité" but now read "Black Lives Matter" and "Love is Love".

It was perfect.

Wordlessly, I handed it back, trying to form words.

"It's...wow. Kit, I mean. God," I stammered, willing myself to stop speaking. She laughed infectiously, edging back onto the stool.

"Of course you'd like the history ones. Dani loves that piece, she subtitled it a 'middle finger to the white patriarchy', or..something along those lines."

I would never get sick of watching Kitty talk about Daniela. It was as though everything else faded away and all she could think about was how much she loved her. Kitty never appeared stressed or saddened, not back then. She always seemed carefree, and yet when Dani was mentioned she lost tension I didn't even know she had. Watching her talk always made me feel a little empty, no matter how much joy it gave me.

That's the thing about loneliness, I suppose. When you're alone - totally alone - being lonely is expected. It would be surprising if you weren't lonely. But when you're surrounded with friends, when you're constantly with people and yet you *still* feel lonely? That stings.

I don't think I truly realised how lonely I was at the time, happy to just be surrounded by these magical people. It's only looking back that I realised I spent those years waiting to be left behind.

I live my life in retrospect.

(I've always been a model history student)

My parents phoned for the first time that week. It really threw me, seeing their names appear on my phone. It wasn't that I had forgotten about them, as such, but they had certainly not been on my mind. I went about those first few weeks in a bit of a daze, taken away by all the changes that I was experiencing. My life at home seemed as though it was a different world. As though it happened to a different person.

The conversation was short and stilted. My father asked after my lectures, making sure I knew he thought history was a waste of time. I could have easily taken the heat off of myself by mentioning the subjects the others took - if my father turned up his nose at history, I couldn't imagine he'd look too kindly upon literature, art, drama and photography - but I would never do that. I don't think I could have dealt with him insulting them. So I listened to him talk about the uselessness of history and resisted the urge to fight back. My mother fretted over whether I was eating enough, and whether I was doing my washing; I bit back the retort that I had been doing my own washing since I was eight whilst she was out having coffee with her friends. I don't remember which excuse I used to get off the phone as quickly as possible, but I know for certain there was one. When I finally made my way back into the kitchen, Kitty laughed at the way I stormed in, pushing a coffee in my hand. She probably made a joke about me needing a trauma blanket. It sounds like something she would say.

By the end of the week, Kitty's studio was opened up for everyone to see. I don't believe she ever realised how impressive the concept of having an entire exhibition dedicated to your work truly was, but to me it was everything. I spent my whole life studying the actions of others - the idea of people paying to come and see my work seemed less something I could achieve, and more the achievements of those I studied. In the light of day, it was even easier to see the true genius behind Kitty's style, rather than in the dusty clutter of her studio. Like I've already said - I know very little about art. Yet even I can understand how stunning her work was.

"I've never understood how she can physically do this much work. She only has 24 hours in the day too, right?" Louis muttered to me, squinting to read one of the descriptions of a painting - it was based off one of Daniela's tattoos, if I'm remembering correctly. It was a common complaint of Louis' - he never seemed to understand how much people could truly do with a day.

"I think you're forgetting that this is Kit we're talking about. You know - Katherine 'my bloodstream is more coffee than blood' Winters? And anyway, she's probably done four hours before you even wake up. It's amazing what someone can do with 24 hours when they don't spend 22 of them asleep," I teased, bumping him with my shoulder. It was a well known fact that Louis would willingly spend all day in bed if it was practical. Some might be annoyed by it, but to me it was just endearing. He was always so calm and peaceful, all soft edges and sleepy smiles. It was why he got on so well with Soph, I think. Alec and Kitty were so fiery, full of energy and ready to explode at any minute. Louis and Sophie, however, lived on a different wavelength. They could go hours without saying a word, perfectly happy with living within their own thoughts. Louis seemed like the only person who truly understood

Soph; we all tried, but I think we were all just too different. Louis, however, understood people.

I just wish we'd understood him.

Louis' favourite piece in the gallery was one of Northam itself. I think it had probably been painted shortly before I came - it looked like autumn, judging off the trees in the background. It was the corner of one of the side buildings - hardly remarkable - but Louis always loved it. The most interesting part about being friends with an artist was being able to see Kitty's life within the paintings. I was able to recognise places she'd painted; her room, the library, the park bench that she'd hid on whenever she felt homesick. Come to think of it, I've always loved finding places I knew; it was as if I could only properly understand a story once I'd been there. I lived through other people's lives.

As I told you: I'm a model history student.

There was one painting which truly stood out, not because it was necessarily my favourite (Liberty Leading the People could never be beaten for me), but because it was such a shock. It was one of those paintings which as soon as I saw it, I stopped, frowned, and took a step backwards. Right in the middle of the central wall was a painting of Sophie. I say painting - it was hard to tell, based on how realistic it was. Her hair was plaited around her head, curls falling softly across her bare shoulders, gently brushing her collarbone. She was staring into the distance and her hair had flowers threaded through it, bursting with purples and blues. For the third time this week, I was rendered speechless by Kitty's artwork.

Here's the thing about my relationship with Sophie up until that point. I loved her, of course I did. I loved her gentle smile and the way she had a clever wit which was even funnier coming from her because she was so mild-mannered. I loved her as I loved them all, but I'd always felt rather distant from her. I suppose she just took a while to properly connect with.

I found this connection looking at Kitty's painting.

It was as though I'd seen her in a whole new way. I think I used to treat her as though she was breakable, as though I needed to watch my words around her in case I say something to hurt her. And a friendship where one is always scared to hurt the other can never work - that's what I've realised over the years. Looking at the painting was the first time I'd seen her as confident. Strong. She seemed to be staring at me, almost challenging me to fight her. She looked even more like Louis; beyond the hair colour and the soft smile, she had the same challenging excitement in her eyes. The thing I loved most about Louis was that he was undoubtedly and inherently kind-hearted, and yet there was always a surprisingly cutting comment just waiting to be made. Kitty's painting made me recognise this quality in Sophie. It was as if, all of a sudden, the two were combined.

I'd never look at Sophie in the same way again.

CHAPTER FOUR

"Love is a smoke raised with the fume of sighs;

Being purged, a fire sparkling in lovers' eyes"

- *Romeo and Juliet*

There were many benefits to living with arts students; I'm sure I've already said more than enough about how they introduced me to living life rather than just studying those who do. And yet during that first year, I very quickly realised that they knew nothing about exam stress.

That was how Soph and I - the only two unfortunate enough to have actual exams - ended up barricading ourselves in the kitchen, buried under flashcards and textbooks. They weren't my first experience with formal exams - far from it - but something in that first term had changed in me. It was as if being surrounded by successful people pushed me to try harder, be better. There's nothing like the threat of being outshined which encourages you to shine brighter.

I said before that I spent the whole friendship waiting to be left behind. Maybe that's what pushed me to be better, trying to get rid of any excuse they could possibly find to do so. I still feel guilty for how badly I misjudged them all. I'd like to say they ever gave me even the slightest reason to doubt their love for me, even if it was just to ease my own guilt, but in truth they did nothing of the sort.

When it all fell apart, there was never once a sense that I was worth less than them, except inside my own mind. I think my thoughts poisoned the reality - that they loved me, and I loved them. Without question. Without reason.

I'm getting ahead of myself again. Back to exam week. I think I went through that week fuelled purely by coffee and stress. As I've already said - it was only Sophie and I who actually had anything to study for; Kitty's gallery show and Alec's play had already counted towards their final grades, and Louis' exhibition was scheduled for a few weeks time. I don't think I actually remember when or how

Dani passed - I don't actually think I ever saw her do any work in our whole time there. Either way, I think it was the longest time I went whilst living in Northam that I didn't see the whole group. Other than Soph, I saw everyone only in passing; Kitty came in once a day to sigh in despair at the dent we were making in her coffee supplies, and Alec could vaguely be heard shouting at the TV in the next room over. I don't remember seeing Louis awake, only ever seeing him curled up in bed as I walked past his room. Every time I did, I couldn't help but smile at his incapability at closing the door. It was just one of those habits we all seemed to love about each other, like Sophie's way of re-plaiting her hair when upset, or Kitty's habit of smudging her eyeliner everywhere.

I learnt a lot about Soph's habits that week, given that we spent so much time holed up studying together. We tested each other on quotes and dates, we shared microwaved noodles and cheese toasties, we even held hands whenever the stress got too overwhelming. I think she properly started to open up around me, letting herself laugh a little louder and for a little longer. Instead of just nodding in reply, she started adding her own comments here and there.

"Battle of Stoke Field?" she asked me once, as I was busy making coffee.

"June 1487," I replied easily - I've always been good at dates.

"You know, I think we've tested each other so much these last few weeks, we could probably sit each other's exams. I mean...okay. What's the quote from Shrew Act 2 Scene 1 which is an example of stichomythia?"

Without hesitation, and despite never actually studying the text, I immediately replied.

"Who knows not where a wasp does wear his sting? In his tail. In his tongue. Whose tongue?"

I glanced at her over my shoulder; she smiled. We both hesitated before bursting into laughter, holding onto my ribs as I laughed. I remember it felt good, laughing.

"God...I think we're going crazy locked up here. Want to get some fresh air?"

I followed her out into the courtyard, taking a seat on the curb and lighting up a cigarette. Sophie watched me, shaking her head with a soft smile.

"'Let's go out for fresh air,' he said, as he lights a cigarette and ruins the fresh air," she said mockingly, sitting next to me. I didn't comment, merely offering her the cigarette and laughing as she spluttered.

"Oh, to be a cigarette, knowing I can cause so much damage without losing the person I need. Relying on others for light whilst hurtling towards the inevitable conclusion: burning out."

I frowned, running through all the texts I'd helped her study in our revision sessions, failing to place the quote.

"Who wrote that?"

Soph smiled at me, a sort of sad and wistful smile.

"Me."

I don't remember how I responded to that. Soph had a way of doing that - rendering me speechless.

After that morning, I started seeing just how much stress I was putting myself under. I think it started with shaky hands, making me struggle when pouring the coffee. Or maybe it was the way that I was finding it just slightly harder to fall asleep, spending longer tossing and turning in bed.

I reached the 'inevitable burning out' stage that Soph had spoken to me about three days before my first exam. It had been a long night of tearing my hair out over Ancient Egyptian source analysis, and something inside of me just died. Or maybe death isn't the right word - if it had died, I wouldn't have been able to feel it, surely. This I could most definitely feel. It felt like something was lodged in my throat, or something was burning deep in my stomach. I don't really remember much other than the overwhelming sense of panic.

Actually, I'll tell you what I do remember. For some reason, there was a quote that was bouncing around my head, even though I couldn't place it.

"Any moment might be our last. Everything is more beautiful because we're doomed. We will never be here again."

I don't even remember where I first read it. I just know that it was the only thing drowning out the repetitive cycle of "you're a failure and they'll all leave you" that was going around my head in a dizzying fashion. I remember Louis finding me a few hours into my spiral. He didn't say anything - or maybe he did, I don't remember - but his steadying hand on my shoulder was enough to calm my breathing. He offered me a sad but hopeful smile when I finally glanced up at him, and that too made everything easier. He wordlessly handed me a glass of water, squeezing my hand again. It was almost as though he was proud of me, I just didn't know for what. Either way, he saved me that night. He offered me the calm I needed, as though he was pulling me through the panic. He guided me to bed, looking as though he wanted to stay. Instead, he simply nodded again before leaving, forgetting to close the door as always.

We will never be here again.

It was also during that first exam season that I spent my first day out with someone outside of Northam. A handful of us from the history course went to the museum together to look through an exhibition on the Victorians, studying together in the park afterwards. It was strange, spending time with people outside of my group. That isn't to say it wasn't enjoyable - I had a good day out and actually got to know the people I'd been attending classes with all this time - but it was eye-opening to say the least. It was the first day where I didn't sit back and realise just how odd my life was now. It felt normal and mundane, but refreshing all the same.

Needless to say I survived the exams. Every day for two weeks I made the endless walk down to the exam hall and prayed I'd done enough. Nobody ever said anything, but there seemed to be an unspoken agreement that Sophie and I were to be looked after that week. The kitchen had never been tidier, and there were always meals prepped and left on the side. I think - I hope - I've made it clear that we were more than just flatmates, more than just friends even. We were family, and family looks after each other. Perhaps it took me a little longer than most people to work that out, given that I only realised this shortly after my 19th birthday. Most people grow up in a family that makes them feel safe, make them feel at home. I don't resent my parents for failing to give that to me. It just meant I had to find my family, my home elsewhere. I found it in a theatre a few roads away from campus, watching my friend yell his lines. I found it in a tiny, overcrowded studio with my head full of paint fumes. I found it on a curb outside my building, listening to a beautiful girl speak poetry about cigarettes. I found it in the music written by my friend, and I found it on the grass after a party. I found it curled up on the kitchen, laughing until my lungs ached and I choked on my coffee.

I found home in the lens of a camera.

We celebrated the end of exams in true Northam fashion; with a themed party. Alec, as always, came up with the theme - this time it was Ancient Greece. I remember his excitement as he worked out everyone's character, putting hours of research into matching their personalities perfectly. I knew very little about greek mythology, so the symbolism went completely over my head except for Alec's own character - Apollo. Even I couldn't miss that one, and joined everyone in the mutual eye roll when he announced it. Dani and Kitty were Muses and Aphrodite respectively, and judging by their laughter it was a good match. Or maybe it was unrelated - we all laughed a lot back then. Sophie was given Hestia, and when I gave her a blank look she merely shrugged.

"Peace and domesticity. There are worse things to be known for."

"Sebastian my good fellow, you get to be Patroclus, and of course curly hair over there is Achilles," Alec announced, and the room went quiet for a second. Kitty was visibly trying not to laugh, and Dani muttered a soft "holy shit." I raised an eyebrow, looking over to Louis in confusion. He just shook his head, giving me a soft smile.

"Don't worry about it Seb. Just a silly joke. Go get ready for the party, it's being thrown for you and Soph anyway."

The costumes this time were a lot simpler to create, simple bed sheets and sandals. Louis painted all of our faces with gold glitter, and Kitty plaited the girls' hair with gold ribbon. Even our drinks were glittery, shimmering in the glasses. In short, it was beautiful.

I said earlier on that they all put a lot of effort into party decorations at Northam. There is no greater illustration of this than at this party. At the entrance of the house, Alec had somehow set up a fake white marble plinth, just like the statues of the Greek gods. Kitty and Dani had decorated it with fake leaves and gold ribbon, fairy lights giving it a bright glow. Louis spent the first half an hour of the party photographing us all on the plinth, and they're some of the most beautiful photos I've ever seen. Sophie's hair looked stunning with the gold ribbons threaded through her plaits, and Kitty's eyes seemed even more green with the gold coating her eyelashes. Alec was clearly imitating the famous statues, a look of confidence on his face that was truly unmatched. Dani's tattoo was visible in the gaps of her make-shift toga, the roses perfectly fitting the theme. Even the photo of me was impressive, Louis somehow managing to make my expression look thoughtful and mysterious, instead of just camera-shy and tipsy. I think this was the party that truly lived up to the belief that Northam was magical - I wish I'd spent more time capturing just how beautiful everyone looked.

I think it was around about my fifth glass of glittery alcohol that I staggered out into the courtyard, skirting past a very drunk Louis dancing in the corner. I loved it when Louis got drunk - he was so pure and childish, dancing around in a circle on his own. I would have stayed and danced with him, but his spinning was making me dizzy and the last thing I needed was to throw up on him. Instead I pushed my way outside and took a deep breath as the cold air hit me, trying to stay on my feet.

"Seb, you good?"

I turned around, leaning heavily against the wall. Soph was sat on the curb again, watching me with an amused smile as I staggered over and landed heavily next to her.

"I'm good, I'm...I'm great! We're great!" I announced loudly, giggling as I did so. She didn't reply, laughing softly into her glass and staring straight ahead.

She had gold dust on her cheekbone and her plaits were unravelling, the blond curls falling past her shoulders. I was once again struck by the resemblance between her and Louis; with her hair pinned up like this it was even more striking.

"You have a really nice smile, Seb. You should smile more often," she whispered, finally turning to look at me. Her cheeks were flushed - with the alcohol, perhaps, or maybe the cold. Still to this day, I don't know what possessed me to do it, denial probably, but I reached out and pulled her towards me. Our lips met and I instinctively ran my hand through her hair, tangling my fingers with the ribbon. She pulled away after a few seconds, mouth agape. She glanced nervously at the ground before giving me the same sad smile.

"You don't want this, Seb. That's okay."

I frowned, shaking my head slightly. She was right, of course, but at the time I had no idea what she meant. She smiled again, reaching up and brushing some of the confetti out of my hair. She looked me in the eyes again, still smiling.

"Patroclus," she whispered, before standing, walking back into the house. I gently touched my lips, confused about what had just happened. It turns out she knew me better than even I did.

By the time I'd made my way back into the party, the guests had left and it was just the six of us again.

"Seb...Sebby...Bas..." Alec slurred, reaching out and gesturing me over. I staggered over to him, letting myself be pulled into a huge hug. I smiled into the embrace, patting him on the head before falling back on the floor again. Everyone laughed, all too giddy off the dangerous glittery drinks. I glanced around and was struck with a feeling of disbelief - how lucky I was to know them all. I still can't believe it, if I'm truthfully honest. Even despite everything, I still truly, honestly, undoubtedly believe it was the greatest honour of my life to be able to spend even part of my existence with them.

Looking back….I think that was the last good day we had before the cracks started to show.

CHAPTER FIVE

"I wasted time, and now doth time waste me;

For now hath time made me his numbering clock:

My thoughts are minutes; and with sighs they jar"

- *Richard II*

There was one last event before the Christmas break - Louis' exhibition. I remember spending those weeks in a sense of suspended dread - the holidays were quickly approaching and I had no idea what they would bring. I think I was too scared to ask if anyone was staying at Northam like I was in case I received exclusively negative answers. I was terrified to be left behind as they flew back to their homes, leaving me in mine.

It was hard to focus on the upcoming holidays though, with the hurricane that was Louis constantly sweeping through the house. He was in a frenzy of photographs, desperately trying to find inspiration. Each morning I would wake up to the sound of his printer whirring in the room next door, and each night I would fall asleep to the sound of a rubber ball hitting the door - a sign I would soon come to realise meant he was stressed. It felt as though he was unable to see anything without first looking at it through the lens, and it was hard for me to watch. I missed him.

It didn't help that Sophie hadn't properly looked me in the eye since the night of the post-exam party. It wasn't as though we had actually fallen out, but it simply felt as though we had been knocked slightly out of orbit. We still spoke in the kitchen and walked to lectures together but it was as though we were simply going through the motions of friendship. Without her and Louis' steadfast kindness, it felt as though the whole house was louder, more chaotic. That's what happens when Kitty and Alec are in charge, I suppose.

I feel I'm painting too much of a bleak picture here, and that isn't quite true. We all still loved each other, and it was still some of the best months of my life. Never doubt that. Even now, I'm overwhelmed by how much love I was capable of having.

There was one afternoon, about a week or two before Louis' exhibition, where we felt properly connected again. At the time he was centering his exhibition around people, wanting to try and capture people's personalities through simple vignettes. Despite the fact that he could barely walk across campus without receiving an offer to model for him, he was only interested in us. This was how we all ended up on the steps outside the house, being photographed doing everyday things which apparently, for Louis, was anything but normal. There's no way I can possibly remember the hundreds of photos taken that day, but some are still burned in my mind. There was a close up of me smoking, cheeks hollow as I blew the smoke out, my eyes closed. One of Kitty swinging around the bannister, mouth open as she laughed. Dani throwing a middle finger at the camera, obscuring most of her face. One of Soph replaiting her hair, tucking it behind her ear. Alec laying across the stairs, head resting on his arm as he stared up at the sky.

I think my favourite one was actually an accident, merely Louis trying to adjust the light settings on the camera. It's imperfect, his thumb obscuring the corner, barely any of us looking towards the lens. I might not be remembering this correctly, I haven't seen the photo in the longest time, but I think Kitty was crouched behind Dani, leaning against her shoulder as she listened to Alec speak. I can't even remember what Sophie was doing, probably biting her nails or laughing at Alec's story. It perfectly captured exactly who we were deep down.

In the photo, I was staring up at Louis with a quiet smile.

It was also that week that Louis first mentioned it. He was flicking through the photos from the week before, a small frown on his face.

"The same guy is in like...twenty of these photos," he muttered, shuffling through them. I didn't really pay him much attention, merely humming and turning my attention back to my paper. He continued to look through them all, his frown deepening.

"So? He was probably doing errands or whatever, you just didn't notice him at the time," I finally muttered, when his sighs had become too distracting to ignore. He glanced up at me, slowly relaxing as he met my eyes. I remember his small laugh, nodding as he rolled his eyes at himself.

"Yeah, yeah - you're probably right. It won't mean anything."

I'd genuinely thought that was the end of it.

God, how I wish that had been the end of it.

By this point we were quickly approaching Louis' exhibition, which meant Kitty was in full 'supportive friend' mode. She was always cooking for Louis, offering to hand out flyers for him, making sure he got enough sleep (for the first time since meeting him, this was actually becoming a problem for Louis). It was as though everyone felt we had all been slightly off recently, and so she was making a special effort to prove we were a family still. Or maybe Kitty just truly cared that much, all the time.

The day finally came, and we all piled into the exhibition space. The first thing which struck me was the sheer number of photos covering the walls. Of course I knew Louis took countless photos but this was his entire life, documented on the walls. I could track exactly where he'd been and who he'd seen; mostly completely common place but seemingly beautiful through his camera. I walked around the space slowly, completely taken by the beauty he'd managed to capture.

"It's pretty impressive, huh?"

I turned to see Sophie staring up at the wall next to me. It was a collection of photographs of eyes, probably around fifty of them. Mine was definitely in the mix somewhere, lost amongst the collection. Some stood out, especially Kitty's bright green. Daniela's was recognisable because of the eyebrow piercings, and I'd know Sophie's anywhere.

"Do you think he sees everything in this level of detail? I mean...do you think everything he sees has a deeper meaning?"

I thought about it for a moment, staring up at the countless eyes on the wall.

"Yeah, I reckon he does. Must be weird to live like that. Beautiful though."

Sophie glanced over and me and shrugged.

"Sounds exhausting to me."

I laughed in surprise, enjoying the sound of her laugh. We stood there for a few minutes, and by the time we parted again all the awkwardness had melted away. It was as though all we needed was a brief moment of happiness for everything to just realign.

Louis spent most of the exhibition loitering in the corner by the photos from around the village. He smiled whenever someone came to congratulate him, but other than that he seemed to be distracted. I tried to leave him alone for as long as possible but every time I saw his frown deepened, I lost a little of my resolve. Eventually he seemed to be scowling at the wall, the emotion ugly on his usually calm and loving face, and I knew I couldn't ignore it any longer. As soon as he saw me coming towards him he carefully rearranged his face, trying to smile at me.

"Hey, how's it going? Are you enjoying it? Quite a few people have commented on the one of you smoking, you make a good subject."

"What's wrong?" I asked outright. I could practically see the nervous energy bouncing off him and knew if I didn't get him to tell me straight away we would be trapped in a whirlpool of platitudes. He struggled to answer at first, before finally letting out a breath and staring at me intensely.

"That man, he's in so many of the photos. I didn't realise at first but I think he's following me, he's everywhere Seb."

I remember thinking it was just the stress of the exhibition which had caused this obsession. I remember just laughing it off, maybe even making a comment about him going crazy. I didn't take it seriously in the slightest.

It's one of my biggest regrets.

CHAPTER SIX

"At Christmas I no more desire a rose

Than wish a snow in May's new-fangled mirth;

But like of each thing that in season grows.

So you, to study now it is too late"

- *Love's Labour's Lost*

In the end, three of us stayed at Northam for Christmas. Kitty never really spoke about her family, merely shrugged and said she didn't get on with them, and would rather stay with her friends and her studio. Alec initially didn't tell us why he wasn't going home - we later found out his parents were going on some fancy cruise in the Mediterranean; we were always mocking Alec for how posh his family was, no matter how much he tried to hide it. The day a letter arrived for 'Alexander Von Rosenberg' will go down in history.

Saying goodbye to the other three was odd. It was jarring to be reminded that they had lives outside of these walls; I suppose that's what happens when you spend so much time with someone. It hadn't actually been that long but already my life seemed to revolve around these people, and so it felt wrong to all of a sudden have three weeks with only half the group. It felt strange to not hear Daniela's music blasting through the walls, and the kitchen seemed tidier without piles of Soph's books on every surface.

One thing that truly made me smile was watching Louis as he left. He threw his bag over his shoulder, propped his suitcase against the wall and pulled the door closed behind him. He glanced up and saw me watching him, smiling before pushing the door open again and walking away. It would have felt wrong to have it closed.

From what I remember, the first few days of the holidays were spent locked in our rooms catching up on sleep. The term time was so active that we were powered by pure adrenaline, and so when we paused even for a second, we crashed. I would pass a sleepy Alec in the corridor on my way towards the bathroom but other than that we used that first weekend to recharge. I didn't think, talk or look at anything to do with history for over 72 hours and it was perfect.

When we finally emerged from our self-imposed hibernation, I realised just how different Kitty and Alec were when they were allowed to just *exist*. Louis and Soph lived their life in a calm, thoughtful, peaceful manner, taking time to think everything through. Kitty and Alec, on the other hand, were constantly active, operating on a high frequency not unlike a hurricane. I only realised on this first break, however, that the latter two could operate on a much calmer level, it was just that they - like I - were spurred on by failure. Only when given permission to relax could they actually slow down and be themselves.

This was how I found them that first morning where we properly started the holidays - calm. Both were slumped at the kitchen table, chatting about something or other. Kitty offered me a sleepy smile as I poured my coffee and joined them at the table, offering me half her bacon sandwich.

"Did the others get back home okay?" she asked, glancing at Alec's phone. He nodded, leaning back in his chair.

Everything that day and indeed, most of the days, were spent in such a mundane fashion that it hardly bears describing. I'll skip ahead to one of the first days we ventured outside Northam. It was the week of Christmas I think, maybe the 20th, 21st perhaps. For once Alec seemed desperate to get out of the house, and after an hour of convincing he finally managed to get Kitty and I on board too. For some reason we made our way down the valley towards the old theatre, taking the long route through the trees. It was quite beautiful to watch Kitty skip down the path, her jet black hair a sharp contrast to her red jacket- or should I say *my* red jacket. That was another one of Kitty's quirks; she was always stealing other people's clothes. If it had been anyone else I imagine it would have been annoying, but this was Kitty. She got away with so much because of how much we all loved her.

Neither of us asked how Alec managed to get himself keys to the theatre, but soon we found ourselves standing on the empty stage, facing the empty audience I was so often part of.

We so often said Alec's demeanor changed when he was on stage. It was as though he was truly at home, like Kitty in her studio. He seemed relaxed yet confident, barely even paying attention to the countless seats. We all sat on the edge of the stage, enjoying having the empty space to ourselves. After a moment or two of quiet Alec stood - he always did struggle with silence.

"So, Miss Katherine, Mr Sebastian, your challenge - if you wish to accept - is to stand right...here," he stood very pointedly in the exact centre of the stage, arms out wide. "And yell the most basic, famous, overused, even-ten-year-olds-know-this-crap Shakespeare quote you've ever heard. Really yell it."

I had to hide the nerves I felt at the thought of making so much noise and being so … out there. As I've already said, I wasn't the centre of my own story. I wasn't the sort of person who acted, I wasn't the sort of person who people wrote about. I was the person who read about those people. It felt wrong to be the one on stage, even in an audience of nobody. Even so, I stood up, watching Alec stand at the front.

"To be or not to be, that is the question!"

He threw us a smug grin, laughing as Kitty punched him on the shoulder.

"Jackass, you know that was mine. Okay...Romeo! Romeo! Wherefore art thou Romeo?"

Her voice was so loud it bounced off the walls, echoing around the empty space. She bowed, pushing me forward. It was stupid how nervous I was, despite there being no audience. In fact, I think it would have been easier acting for actual people; at least then any judgement thrown my way would be valid, instead of just a figment of my own self doubt.

"All the world's a stage, and all the men and women merely players."

It was met with silence, and when I glanced at the other two they rolled their eyes.

"Wow Seb, even I barely heard that. I said yell it!"

I repeated the line again, glancing over at them again and receiving a shake of their heads.

"I think you maybe reached the second row there mumbles. C'mon, take a deep breath, relax your shoulders, and really shout it. There's nobody here. Just let it go."

I followed his instructions, raising my gaze to look towards the upper circle.

"ALL THE WORLD'S A STAGE, AND ALL THE MEN AND WOMEN ARE MERELY PLAYERS"

I heard my own voice echo around me, mixing with the cheers from the other two. I couldn't help the grin that broke out across my face, giving a fake bow to the empty audience.

That was when we heard the door open from one of the wings. Alec reacted first, letting out a string of curses as he jumped off the stage.

"It's the bloody Chancellor, run," he muttered, legging it down the aisle. Kitty laughed incredulously as she pushed me towards the edge of the stage, both running from the protests we were having shouted at us. We didn't stop running until we'd reached the steps to Northam, collapsing down as we tried to catch our breath.

"Alexander von Rosenberg, you little shit. Are you trying to get us kicked out?" Kitty asked, her harsh words undercut by her hysterical laughter. We sat on the steps for the longest time, breathing heavily and coming down from the adrenaline rush. As much as I missed the others, there was something nice about it being quieter around the house, or as quiet as it can get with Alec and Kit. It gave me time to realise just how much of a family we'd truly become - nothing makes you realise how much you rely on someone until they're gone. This is a lesson I couldn't possibly grasp until later on.

I got a phone call from Louis on Christmas eve. I didn't think anything of it when I first saw his name show up on the phone; he hadn't called all holiday, but we'd spoken to all the others now and then. I answered fairly quickly, worried about the ringtone waking up Kitty and Alec. It was fairly late, everyone exhausted from our late night game of Twister.

"Louis - happy Christmas eve!" I replied, and was met with a tired sigh.

"Hey Seb," he muttered, and I immediately frowned. Before I could ask him what was wrong, he cut me off.

"What have you been up to?" I paused, and he sighed again. "Please Seb, just...just talk to me? How are Alec and Kitty?"

I remember he seemed tired, desperate for me to just talk at him. I could understand that; whenever I was overwhelmed, I often just wanted to sit there and have someone's words wash over me.

"Okay, um. Oh, I have a classic Alec story to tell you," I began to tell the story of the other day at the theatre, and I could almost hear him relaxing as I spoke. At the start of the conversation I could feel the tension through the phone, but the more I said the more he began to reply, laughing at my stories, adding a comment here and there. By the time I ran out of things to say, we'd reached a comfortable silence.

"So, how are you?" I asked after a while, almost worried to hear the answer. There was a pregnant silence and I could practically hear the walls going up again.

"Seb...I think-" he broke off, and even in the dark of my room I raised my eyebrow.

"Nevermind. It's nothing."

"No, go on. What's wrong?" I stammered, desperate for him to finally open up about what had clearly been bothering him these last few months.

"Nothing. It's nothing. Have a good Christmas, Seb. Love you."

He hung up, and I sat in the dark for what felt like forever.

I don't think, at the time, I even registered the last thing he'd said.

By the time Christmas morning came around, the weather outside had become so bad we had little choice but to stay inside under blankets. It was sort of a perfect day actually - Christmas at home had meant traipsing down to church in our finest clothes before spending dinner having stilted conversation with distant relatives. Whilst it was a big adjustment going from that to sitting in our pyjamas in the kitchen, eating noodles and chicken nuggets, it felt right. We played cluedo and monopoly, we got drunk and we sang christmas carols at an obnoxiously loud volume. It was that night we took one of the only photos I have taken by someone other than Louis - it was the three of us under a blanket, looking sleepy. We were quite a few glasses of wine in by that point, and you could tell. Kitty was laying with her head in my lap, grinning at the camera with shining eyes. I was absentmindedly stroking her hair, head tilted backwards as though I was half asleep. Alec was in the corner, just a glimpse of hair and flushed cheeks, trying to take the photo with himself in it. It was imperfect - slightly blurry with an awkward framing, but it was honest. It perfectly captured the moment in a way so many photos fail to do.

Talking of photos, we'd received many from the others over the holiday. The first one that had come was from Louis - it was a photo of the train station. Stations always made me emotional for some strange reason; I think it's because their very existence signified leaving a place, moving on. You could truly go anywhere, be anyone. I found that idea more and more appealing as the years went on.

Sophie sent a photo taken on Christmas day - her normally plaited hair was loose and she was holding a tiny kitten up towards the camera. She'd attached a short note, introducing us to Ariel and wishing us all a happy Christmas. We'd spent ages cooing over the kitten - until we pointed out that with her green eyes and jet black fur, she resembled Kitty far more than a cat should do. I suppose it made sense, with the name and all.

Daniela's photo came much later than everyone else - it was simply a photo of herself on a beach back home in Puerto Rico. I wanted to be jealous of the sun and the heat, but being realistic it would have burned my pale, freckled skin within seconds. She was beaming and whilst I couldn't be entirely sure, I thought I noticed a few new tattoos scattered across her collarbone.

We taped the photos up on the fridge and I found myself counting down the days until they returned. I had loved getting to spend the holidays with just the three of us, but I found myself craving the return of the whole group. Louis and Sophie's absence had hurt more than I realised, and despite nearly three weeks passing since they'd left, I'd still found myself glancing through Louis' open door, expecting to see him lying there, curled around the blanket with his curls going haywire.

As for Sophie, now that we had salvaged our friendship after the awkward kiss incident, I found myself valuing her company even more than before. Throughout the holidays she sent me photos of anything she came across that was vaguely historical - a blue plaque in her village, a sign at a local English Heritage Site, various museum exhibitions. It made me unreasonably happy to know she was thinking about me. It made me feel validated, less unforgettable.

The date came when the holidays ended and term time started up again. People started gradually moving back into the house, and I watched as they slowly arrived. Daniela, jumping up and throwing her arms around Kitty as soon as she arrived. Sophie, beaming as she held out the kitten for us all to see.

I wish I could end the story here.

God. How I wish this was the end.

CHAPTER SEVEN

"Now cracks a noble heart.

Good-night, sweet prince;

And flights of angels sing thee to thy rest."

- *Hamlet*

It took a week.

It took a week of looking anxiously out of the window, wondering where he was. It took a week of frantic phone calls and attempts to contact his family to find out where he was. A week of Sophie biting her lip and glancing nervously at the news. A week of my heart racing every time the door opened.

And then, all of a sudden, Louis was back. I walked in after a lecture to find him sitting in the kitchen like nothing had happened. He didn't explain where he'd been, merely shrugging and making some non-committal noise. I tried my hardest to take the win; after all, I had him back.

I was naive to think everything would just go back to normal.

Because the truth is, Louis never really returned. Not as himself, anyway. He pretended like everything was fine, but his smile didn't reach his eyes. He spent too much time staring off into the distance, fingers gently tracing his lips in deep thought. I don't think I saw him take a photo for at least a week.

It really started to hit me just how deeply changed he was when I did my customary glance into his room and saw his bed scattered with photographs. I recognised them as the ones from the exhibition - the ones with the man in the background. They were creased and some were torn slightly, as though he had been obsessively flicking through them all. I think it was then that it began to sink in that Louis hadn't let it go, not in the slightest. This obsession with the man was consuming him, burning him out. I felt lost. I didn't even know if he'd mentioned this to the others, and I certainly didn't want to drag more people into it than needed.

The truth is, not once did I actually worry about the man in the photographs. I still haven't. I never believed it was anything more than an odd coincidence, and even after all these years I still can't believe there was any darker motive. That wasn't to say he was harmless, though. He caused so much harm. He just didn't realise it.

The changes to Louis' demeanor were too much to ignore, however, and everybody noticed it. We all seemed reluctant to voice our concerns, and so it took place in hushed tones in the doorways. We whispered things like "Louis….do you think he's okay? I mean, do you think he…" before we trailed off, too scared to finish the sentence. Kitty would give him tea, squeezing his shoulder and offering a too-bright smile. Nobody *actually* said anything though, and that was where we went wrong. We should have addressed the downfall he'd clearly gone through during the holidays. We should have helped.

Reader...please, if you are ever in the position I found myself in back then, do something. Anything. I can't begin to put into words the guilt I feel over my inability to act. It's the feeling of waking up in the middle of the night with a racing heart, swallowing down the sick feeling and having to close your eyes against the swimming lights surrounding you. It's the feeling where you suddenly have to clench your hands and grit your teeth because you just feel so damn useless.

Do Something.

We were three weeks into term when I sat in my bed one night and reached for my computer. I stared at the empty search bar for the longest time, before slowly typing.

"I think my best friend has gone mad"

I didn't read any of the search results - all seven hundred and sixty-eight million of them. Just typing it felt like I was betraying him.

This isn't to say those weeks were all completely awful. That's just not true. I loved my lectures, and I loved having the house back together again. Kitty and I would have picnics together out on the field, and Alec and I returned on more than one occasion to the theatre, enjoying the feeling of being on stage more and more with each trip. It wasn't all awful, but it was dampened. It was hard to enjoy yourself when a person you love is in so much pain.

This next part is going to be hard to write, even now. You'll have to bear with me.

Over the weeks after christmas, I'd adopted the habit of doing my reading in the kitchen at night, long after everyone had gone to bed. It was easier to concentrate when the only noise was the sound of the fridge humming, the occasional bird outside. Looking back, I think I'd been drowning too. I'd been engulfed by concern for Louis, struggling to focus on anything else. Maybe that was why I craved the night, because I didn't have to hide my worry behind forced smiles. I didn't have to turn away to wipe my eyes whenever I saw him fail to photograph something which before he would have been inspired by.

It was the 3rd of February. I was sitting in the kitchen at about midnight as always, struggling to make sense of 17th Century foreign policy notes. It wasn't necessarily unusual for Louis to join me briefly in the kitchen, and this was one of those nights. He seemed calmer, giving me a small smile as he joined me on the sofa. My heart jumped and I allowed myself the briefest glimmer of hope that maybe he was getting better, maybe this was the end of whatever had engulfed him the last few weeks. The next words out of his mouth proved me wrong.

"The man in the photos is dead."

He said it in a voice almost overspilling with sadness, glancing up at me through his long eyelashes. When I didn't - couldn't - respond, he sighed.

"I tracked him down, that week after christmas. I went around the shops he'd been standing outside in the photos, asked the people inside if they knew him. Eventually somebody gave me a name, and

I tracked down his address. He died the week of christmas, apparently. Liver failure."

If I hadn't known Louis, this would have been good news. I could have tried to suggest that this was for the best - he wasn't in any danger, he could move on. Knowing Louis as I did though, I knew this was the last thing he wanted. Louis has an inherent need to understand the world. It's why he photographed, I think. He wanted to capture everything, document *everything*, so he could grow in his understanding. I said earlier that he always listened intently to everything, giving everyone his full and undivided attention. He wanted to understand people. Losing this man, whoever he was, ended his chances of getting answers. He would never know if it was just a series of coincidences, or whether he was - as he so clearly believed - being followed. It was something he could never understand, no matter how much he tried. I realised now that his demeanor these last few weeks wasn't frantic or desperate, as it had been before the holidays. It was as though he'd given up, like he'd lost the energy to care now that there was something definitive he would never understand.

"You know, Seb. I haven't mentioned any of this to the others, and I don't even know why. I don't know why there's something about you that forces me to open up, but there is. I feel so at home at Northam, and yet there's something truly saddening about this place, don't you agree? I never could put my finger on it. I think it just worries me that I'm so happy here."

This was one of those occasions where my own words failed me, so I fell back on the quote I had relied on so many times since.

'There's something awfully sad about happiness, isn't there?'

He glanced up at me again, his mouth breaking into a shy smile. Without a word, he placed his hand on my shoulder, turning me towards him. Before I truly had a chance to respond, he was kissing me, and I knew what home felt like. I threaded my hand through his hair, instinctively pulling him closer. A million thoughts flew through my mind, but the one that stood out was the same quote that had raced through my mind that night he held me during exams.

"Any moment might be our last. Everything is more beautiful because we're doomed. We will never be here again."

I still had no idea where I knew it from, but it felt poignant. For a brief second I allowed myself to imagine life after that night, but I simply found it wasn't possible. I had no clue what the next day would hold, or the day after.

If I had, would I have held him for longer? Would I have whispered into his ear and promised to never let him go?

Eventually he pulled away, allowing us to finally catch our breaths again. I risked a quick glance at him, and realised he was crying. It pained me to see the painfully red skin under his eyes. He was so beautiful. When he finally looked up at me, he smiled.

"Goodnight, Sebastian."

I watched him walk out of the kitchen, unable to move. I'm unsure of how long I sat there, a stupid smile on my face as I ran my thumb across my lips. Eventually I pulled myself together, turning off the light and walking to bed, lightheaded. I passed his room and felt my heart flutter strangely.

Writing this now, I want to scream at myself. I was missing something so obvious. It's glaringly obvious now, looking back. I live my life in retrospect.

How did I not notice? It was such a simple thing and yet was of such fundamental importance. Current me screams in frustration. It was right there. Right in front of my eyes.

Here's the thing.

I walked down the corridor from the kitchen, passing the bedrooms on my way to my own.

I walked past Louis' room.

His door was closed.

CHAPTER EIGHT

"Parting is such sweet sorrow that I shall say goodnight till it be morrow."

   -   *Romeo And Juliet*

I woke to the sound of Sophie screaming.

It's so wrong that she had to find him. Soph, the most innocent and kind of us all. The one who, more than anything else, I wanted to protect. She shouldn't have been the one to find him.

They said it was an overdose. Sleeping pills. A handful of them.

It shouldn't have been Sophie to find him.

The door was closed. Of course she was going to notice. How would anybody not?

She didn't stop screaming for nearly an hour. Alec had tried to quieten her, holding her to his chest, but the screams were simply muffled. Kitty threw up a few times, I think. I don't really remember. Daniela was the only one of us to react in any way, calling for an ambulance. We stood in that goddamn doorway and just stared. I couldn't take my eyes off him.

Even after they took him, I couldn't move from the doorway. I think someone tried to pull me away, but I couldn't move.

I think it was three hours later when I finally walked into the kitchen. Maybe it was more. Time didn't really seem to have any meaning. Acknowledging the passage of time would mean we were moving on.
We were leaving him behind.

When I appeared in the doorway of the kitchen, I was met with a vignette which made my heart ache. Sophie had stopped screaming finally, but the look of blank desperation was worse. It shouldn't have been her.

Kitty was crying, of course, and she looked smaller than I ever thought was possible. I needed her to laugh, I needed her to tell me this wasn't real. Kitty's tears were ugly, out of place. She spent her life putting beauty into the world and it threw it back at her.

Daniela's face was tucked into the pillow, her whole body shaking. It almost made me dizzy to look at her.

Alec...Alec was trying so hard to be strong, but he was failing so badly. He looked like a lost child, his eyes wide and sad. He looked almost like he was going to get on his knees, begging for a reason why.

"Seb," Kitty whispered, her voice broken in a way that made me sick to my stomach. I barely responded to my own name.

I don't know how much more I can say without losing it.

I'll end this chapter with this last comment. There are very few things I am totally sure of from this time. I wandered about in a cloud of uncertainty, so instead I will tell you three things I do know for sure.

It shouldn't have been Sophie to find him.

The door was closed.

I loved him. I loved him desperately. I loved him without logic and without reason.

How did I not notice the door?

CHAPTER NINE

"My grief lies all within,

And these external manners of lament

Are merely shadows to the unseen grief

That swells with silence in the tortured soul."

- *Richard II*

I had to learn to miss Louis, it didn't come naturally. Firstly, I had to shake off the numb feeling which had engulfed me from the second I had heard Sophie's scream. For about four days I didn't have the energy to feel anything other than numb, and therefore I couldn't miss him. Maybe that was for the best.

Slowly, I began to regain feeling. It was as though I was seeing the house for the first time. He was everywhere. His toothbrush was on the sink next to mine, waiting for him to turn the light on and swear at the sudden brightness.. His hoodie was thrown over one of the kitchen chairs, for when he inevitably got too cold at night. His mug was next to the kettle, waiting for him to stumble into the kitchen and scowl into his coffee until he'd properly woken up. It was as though his entire life had just been put on pause - everything was waiting for him to just walk through the door and carry on like nothing was wrong.

His parents turned up in that first week. I hadn't realised - of course, we knew they would visit soon - and unfortunately I was in the kitchen with them for nearly an hour. As I listened to them talk softly to Kitty and Dani, their voices sounding almost as if it hurt to speak. It made me wonder whether that's why Sophie wasn't speaking - maybe it would simply cause too much pain. I couldn't help but imagine how my parents would have reacted if it was them instead of the Mitchells. The bitter part of me wondered if they would even care.

"It's weird, isn't it Edward? How barely anything here has changed?" Louis' mother commented, glancing up at the room as we walked them down the staircase. I'd vaguely known that his parents had come to the school, but I hadn't realised they'd stayed at Northam. I didn't give it a second thought, though. It took two people who were a product of Northam to give birth to someone so quintessentially intelligent as Louis. I was mostly just grateful that they didn't touch his room, saying that it would be too painful. It felt comforting to know a small piece of Louis was still at Northam, at least.

The school cancelled lectures for the week and bought everyone into the hall, announcing his death and telling everyone that help would be there for anyone who wanted it. None of Northam went. They apparently gave a short speech about Louis, but didn't say much. I think they knew there was nothing they could say that we wouldn't cover in our eulogies.

The first time I thought about the speech was in the kitchen about a week before the funeral. Kitty was sitting on the floor, staring into an empty sketchbook.

"Seb...have you written your eulogy yet? I finished it earlier and I just-"

She broke off, her voice cracking.

"I haven't yet. I probably won't write too much, I'll come up with something on the day I guess," I replied. It wasn't like I'd ever had difficulty talking about Louis.

Kitty just nodded, unable to look up from the floor.

"I can't believe we have to do this," she whispered after minutes of silence. I didn't reply - I didn't need to. None of us could bear the fact we were having to make this speech, and yet none of us would ever entertain the idea of not making one. We owed Louis that.

The only doubt I had lay with Sophie. In the entire week, I think I'd heard her say maybe four or five words in total. She'd been practically silent, as though she'd screamed so much that day she simply couldn't speak anymore. Even she planned to make a speech though; I'd seen her scribbling tearfully into her notepad.

The night before the funeral we all trudged up the hill where we'd slept that night after the 1940s party. I don't really know why we ended up there, but somehow it felt right. We just stood there, looking down the hill towards Northam. I felt a hand grip my shoulder and felt myself being pulled into a group hug. Nobody said anything, but there was a mutual understanding of what was going unsaid. That night I wrestled with myself over how truthful I was going to be at the service tomorrow. Just how truthful could I be?

The funeral was held in the assembly hall on campus, and all the blue and gold signs - the colours of the school - were replaced with black fabric. It took my breath away slightly to see the vast number of people in attendance; all the seats were full, and countless people were standing in the back. By the time we arrived, there were only five empty seats - right at the front, with reserved signs on them. It felt a little twisted - having a reservation for my best friend's funeral. As we took our seats, I felt the eyes of hundreds' on me, burning with pity. The chancellor took to the stage and I felt Sophie's hand slip into mine.

"Good morning. We are, as you all know, gathered here today to celebrate the life of our friend and esteemed student, Louis Mitchell."

As he spoke, I found myself unable to tear my eyes away from the photograph framed on the stage. It was a black and white one of him, turned slightly to the side. He was holding his own camera up to his eyes, a calm smile on his face. I don't know who he was photographing, but it was clear that he was in his element. He looked so peaceful; it was so different to the constant look of worry he'd been showing over the last few months.

God, I missed him.

Sophie squeezed my hand, and I somehow managed to pull myself back into the room.

"I now invite some of Louis' closest friends to come up and speak. The first eulogy will be delivered by Daniela Hernandez."

Dani climbed up on stage, and I watched as she took a shaky breath.

"Good morning, everyone. Thank you for being here. I'm not going to speak for long, I know the others have things to say too. Louis...Louis was one of the gentlest people I've met. So many of you know him as one of the mysterious Northamers, walking around campus photographing random things and people. I'm sure you all thought he was weird, photographing pieces of grass that had no meaning whatsoever. It's okay, you can admit it. I know I did when I first met him. But over time, I realised it was just one of his quirks. It was just another thing to love about him. Louis...I'm sorry we didn't notice something was wrong before it was too late. I'm going to miss you more than I can say, man. I love you."

As she climbed down from the stage and hugged Kitty on her way up, I knew I wasn't the only one crying. Kitty looked shattered, the eyes under her glasses red and swollen. The black jumper she was wearing was too big for her, the sleeves pulled down low over her hands.

"Hi everyone. Um. I'm Kitty Winters, Louis' housemate. I really struggled with what I should say in this, because if I'm being truthful, I don't think I've accepted that this is happening. This is all so wrong. Louis deserved so much better. I know I'll never truly accept or understand why he did this, but I don't think any of us understood Louis. He was a mystery, but that's why we loved him. You know, he was the first friend I ever showed my artwork to. I was terrified about what he would say, I admired his work so much. He didn't ramble about my work, he didn't gush or make some big speech - that simply wasn't Louis' style. Instead, he just sighed, smiled, and closed his eyes. I don't know why that meant so much to me, but there was just something so inherently loving about it. I don't think I ever told him how much that meant to me. Louis, you were my brother in every way that mattered, and I don't know how to accept that you're gone. I love you so much."

Once Kitty had wiped her eyes and climbed off stage, the Chancellor invited Alec to speak. He was introduced by his full name, and despite everything, we all laughed. It was a pathetic and tearful laugh, but it was a laugh all the same.

"Louis was an awful person to live with. I know this doesn't sound like the typical start to a eulogy, but bear with me. He was awful. The kitchen always smelled like burnt toast - the boy couldn't cook to save his life. His endless supply of jumpers would always find their way into my laundry basket, no matter what. He slept most hours of the day and was a nightmare before his first cup of coffee. But here comes the part more fitting for a funeral. Despite this, despite all of his flaws, he was still one of the best people I knew.

He was so wonderfully flawed that I couldn't help but love him. Louis, thanks for everything. You deserved so much better."

There was a pause as Alec climbed off stage, and we all waited to see what would happen. Soph still hadn't spoken unprompted since the day he'd died, and so nobody really knew whether she could make the speech. I squeezed her hand and tried to give her a smile. After a few deep breaths she walked onto the stage, and my hand felt empty. She looked so small, so broken, and all I wanted to do was pull her far away from here, somewhere she would be safe.

When she finally spoke, it was nothing more than a whisper, and everyone leant closer.

"Hello everyone I'm Sophie Wright. I...I struggled to come up with my own speech for today, and so I wanted to just quote a passage from one of my favourite texts. Me and my friends quote a lot of Shakespeare, and I know Louis loved this text."

I smiled; there was nothing more intrinsically Sophie than using other people's words instead of her own.

"Beauty is but a vain and doubtful good; a shining gloss that fadeth suddenly; a flower that dies when it begins to bud; a doubtful good, a gloss, a glass, a flower, lost, faded, broken, dead within an hour." she recited, hugging herself. "Louis found beauty in everything, and he photographed them so he could preserve their place in history. I hope we can do the same for him."

She fell silent, and that was the last time I heard her speak.

My stomach clamped uncomfortably as I stood on shaky legs, making my way across the stage. I watched my hands tremble and I glanced up at the audience, dry mouthed. I thought back to the day during the holidays, where we stood on the stage and faced an empty audience. That day, I'd said it would have been easier to face an actual audience than an empty one, and now here I was, facing an actual audience. It was harder than I could have ever imagined.

"Hello everyone, thank you for coming today to help us celebrate Louis. I'm Sebastian, and Louis was-" *Louis was the love of my life.*

"-one of my closest friends." I couldn't do it. I couldn't be truthful. I glanced down and saw Sophie smile at me; she'd always known. I finally realised what she'd meant that night we'd kissed.

"Louis was the first person I met at Northam, and I knew he was special from that first moment. He had something magical; he had some special talent to capture the beauty in the everyday, and that was what made him beautiful. But most of all, his beauty came from watching him interact with others. He was the greatest friend any of us will ever have. It is the greatest honour of my life to be able to know this group of people, and none more so than him."

I took a deep, steadying breath, glancing down at them all.

"Louis, I'm so sorry I couldn't help you. You were a better man than any of us deserved, my friend."

And then, as I stepped away from the microphone, I whispered one last quote. Nobody but I heard it, but that was okay. Only he needed to hear it.

"Never bury my bones apart from yours"

I collapsed when I finally reached my seat. I don't remember the rest of the service, other than Sophie gripping my arm. I think we went back to Northam; I don't remember walking back.

By the end of the night I'd stopped crying, I think. Sophie still hadn't said a word. Kitty was drunk.

"Never bury my bones apart from yours", said Patroclus to Achilles"

CHAPTER TEN

"When sorrows come,

they come not single spies

But in battalions"

- *Hamlet*

Despite my doubts, life moved on. Slowly.

It took me two weeks to go back to lectures. It was only after a letter from the school which read, essentially, that they were sorry my friend had died, but they could only excuse so much before my attendance became a problem. I'd thought about tearing it up, but Sophie had convinced me not to, with just a hand on my arm and a pointed look - she still hadn't said a word.

Walking back into the classroom that day was like a gladiator walking into the colosseum. All eyes turned to me, following me to my seat. The boy at the desk next to me whispered his condolences; I ignored him. I quickly realised the only way to survive life post-Louis was to limit him to Northam. Life outside had to go on - inside I could break down as much as I wanted, but out here, he had to be left behind. It's the only way I could survive it.

I entered somewhat of a routine. I would wake up, gritting my teeth as I walked past the closed door. It was always going to be closed. Breath. Attend classes; we were studying the American War of Independence, I believe. Make casual conversation with my coursemates. Pretend Louis was at home. Get back home, see his door again. Cry. Repeat the next day. It was an exhausting way of living, but it was what needed to be done.

Every night we would eat dinner together, pointedly ignoring the empty chair at the table. We would make conversation, we would play music and study together, we would pretend like everything was okay.

I think we all threw ourselves into our work a little too hard. Alec could be heard in his room, reciting his lines. They were working on All My Sons, which at the time I knew nothing about. He could be heard ranting at all times of the day, which felt strangely comforting. Nightmares live in silence.

Whilst I threw myself to the books and Alec to the script, Sophie withdrew to her writing. She could be seen scribbling at the table for hours. It was almost as though her mind was racing with thoughts she couldn't say, and so she wrote them down instead. It must be awful, trapped inside your mind like that.

Though, I suppose, her writing was not much different to this.

The exception to the rule was Kitty. Whilst we all used our work to distract us, she seemed to be actively ignoring hers. I don't think I'd seen her go to the studio since Louis' death. I could understand it though - her art was emotive; she reacted to what she was feeling. If I was her, I wouldn't want to put my emotions out into the world when they're that dark and ugly. She lived to create beauty, but there's only so much you can create when you have nothing to start with.

I think it was about a week after the funeral that I heard the front door open whilst I was having my midnight cry in the kitchen. I hate to say it, but a small part of me - the part of me who thought we were all in the flat - sat up a little straighter, heart clenching with hope. It wasn't him, of course. It was Kitty, stumbling in. She saw me and started giggling, throwing herself onto the sofa and resting her head against my shoulder.

"Hey Sebby, how you doing?" she whispered loudly, giving me a childish grin. I could practically smell the alcohol on her, her cheeks bright red from either the cold outside or the drink.

"I've been better. How about you? Do you need some water? Food?" I offered, stroking her hair gently. She shook her head, closing her eyes and wincing.

"-room, it's spinning" she muttered, slowly sitting up with my help. She stayed slumped over for a while, and I could almost feel the energy draining from her.

"Why do you think he did it?" she asked softly, staring at her feet. I didn't reply; I knew the answer, of course, but for some reason I still couldn't bring myself to tell the others about the man. I was saved from giving a response by Dani, who came in, rubbing her eyes tiredly.

"Kit? Have you just got in?" she asked, not getting a reply. She rolled her eyes, looking at me instead.

"She drunk again?"

I nodded, not wanting to get in the middle of the two of them. I could sense an argument brewing, and when Kitty and Dani fought, your best bet of survival was to run in the opposite direction as fast as possible. I was thankful when Dani didn't yell, clearly waiting until Kit was sober. Instead she just helped Kitty up, simply sighing as she pulled her back to their bedroom. The look she gave her - pursed lips and gritted teeth - suggested that this was far from the first time that she had taken care of a drunk Kitty recently.

The next morning, the only indication that anything had happened was the fact that Kitty was falling asleep at the dinner table and Dani wasn't making any attempt to stay quiet. Alec gave me a glance over the table, raising his eyebrow in question. I sighed in response, not wanting to get into it at the table. Who was I to judge Kitty's coping habits anyway?

I was almost thankful when exams rolled around. Just like last term, only Soph and I had exams, but this time was obviously different. I was using the exams as a complete distraction - learning dates was so much easier. I think I was trying to fill my head with so many facts that it wouldn't have room to be filled with my own dark thoughts.

Just like last time, Sophie and I practically locked ourselves in the kitchen to study. In practical terms, it seemed the same. I took over the sofa, textbooks scattered over every surface. Sophie was at the table, stacks of books with hundreds of post-it notes littered throughout. There was the same abundance of half drank coffee cups, the same microwave noodles for every meal. The difference was the silence. It bordered on unbearable - we didn't test each other, and so whilst we technically studied together, I felt more alone than ever before. Instead of waking up to Kitty making us a healthy breakfast, we walked in to see her nursing a hangover and using the last of the coffee.

Sophie's exams started before mine, and so when she came back from her first paper, I made sure there was some food waiting for her.

"How did it go?" I asked, more to fill the silence than anything else. She shrugged in response, giving me a half smile.

"I'm sure it went great, you know your stuff," I replied, handing her the mug of tea and squeezing her shoulder. When I left the kitchen, I felt a little lighter. I stopped at Alec's door, and when he opened I offered to run lines with him. Sitting on his bed, going through the script with him felt normal. For the first time ever, I understood Louis' obsession with the mundane. When you go through something as earth shattering as we did, you learn to value normality. It took me a while to work that out - in fact, it was thanks to my American history notes. I read a sentence about the post-Depression era; Americans valued conservative policies in the 1930s not because it was going to help them prosper, but because it felt safer than trying to change anything. I understood where they were coming from. Helping my friends might not actually make the situation better, but it was a safe option which helped me pretend that life could go on.

My first exam date came around quickly, and I found myself almost enjoying having something else to focus on. The student welfare officer pulled me aside on my way into the hall, telling me that she was aware of the situation, and that it would be taken into consideration during marking. She left me with a sympathetic pat on the shoulder and a quick good luck.

As I sat down and waited for the exam to start, I took a deep breath. I realised I didn't particularly care about my result; I wanted to do well, of course, but at the end of the day I couldn't blame myself for being distracted. Looking back to the days before the funeral, I wouldn't have been able to picture myself ever going to another lecture again, so making it to the final exam seemed like a success in itself.

When I left the exam hall, I felt quietly confident. I'd known how to answer most of the questions, and I'd done it within the time limit. I was planning to head back up to Northam, but on my way up I couldn't help wandering off the path. The campus was built in a valley; the lecture halls and most of the newer accomodation was built near the bottom, with woodland paths leading back up the valley slope. Northam was at the top of the valley, mostly hidden by the trees. Whilst I normally took the main stairs up, today I found myself walking off the path, finding myself on the mud path towards the top. There was no logic or reason for why I decided to take the much longer route, but something was driving me. By the time I made it back to Northam, I was freezing and exhausted, but my head felt clearer than ever before. There was a cup of tea and a sandwich waiting for me on the kitchen table, with a note that read "Seb, hope the exam went well - Soph". Of course the tea was cold due to my detour, but it still warmed me to know she'd been thinking of me.

We reached the end of exams, but there was no suggestion of any form of celebration. Instead, I spent the night awake with Alec, running lines in the kitchen. It went unsaid, but we were both nervously waiting for Kit to come home. She was out again - I still had no clue where she went on these nights out, but they were becoming more and more regular. I could tell Alec was as concerned as I was, but neither of us could bring ourselves to bring it up.

When she finally came in, she wasn't alone. She stumbled into the kitchen, her hand wrapped around some girl's waist. I vaguely recognised her as a media studies student; she had a reputation on campus for being the go-to person for drugs. Kitty pulled her closer, clearly wanting to kiss her. Alec and I exchanged the quickest of glances before leaping up. I pulled Kitty towards the sofa whilst Alec manhandled the girl out of the house, trying to quieten her.

"Seb! Why are you ruining my night?" Kitty cried, gripping the front of my shirt. I didn't reply, handing her a glass of water and closing my eyes, a hand over my face.

When I took it away, my eyes immediately went to the door, where Daniela was standing. I wish she had looked angry. Instead she just looked broken.

The look she gave Kitty nearly shattered me.

CHAPTER ELEVEN

"My tongue will tell

the anger of my heart,

Or else my heart

concealing it will break"

- *The Taming of The Shrew*

To her credit, Dani waited until Kitty had sobered up before she laid into her. I'm not entirely sure what happened during the night - I'd fallen asleep fairly soon after we'd kicked the girl out.

I woke up to the sounds of screaming, and it panicked me to my core. I struggled to take a proper breath for a few moments, fearing that morning was happening all over again. It was only when I realised the screams were out of anger, not fear, that I recalled the events of the night before.

In the hallway, Dani was throwing clothes into a box. Kitty was stood to one side, silent tears rolling down her face as she sobbed into her sleeves. Every now and again she would go to speak, silenced by Dani's angry glare. She softened once she'd packed the box of her things up, sighing and running a hand over her face in exhaustion.

"Look, I get it. I know you're going through the shittiest thing ever. But we all are, okay. I lost my friend too! We're all dying here, but we need to have some hope, some trust it's going to get better, or else what's the point?"

It was wrong to see Dani cry; kind, strong, stable Dani who never let anything get to her. But as she stood there, clearly in pain, it was easy to see she was just as broken as us all.

"I'm so -" Kitty broke off, hiccuping as she sobbed. Soph made a move to hug her, but Kit pushed her away gently. She didn't think she was deserving of Sophie's comfort. That was something I understood more than most.

"I know," Dani replied, in a voice barely more than a whisper. "I know. But I can't sit around and get hurt like this. I won't let you destroy yourself and take me down with you. This isn't forever, I just….I can't stay, not with you like this."

It was heart wrenching to watch her pick up her box of things, walking down the hallway. She paused with her hand on the door handle for the briefest of seconds, and the entire house took a hopeful breath. But then a second later she was gone.

I could never blame Dani for leaving that day. I know Alec resented her a little - I'd heard him complaining about it to Sophie. "Kit's just lost her best friend but it's *Dani* who can't handle it?" is what he'd said. I got where he was coming from, but in truth I was angry at Kitty too. I didn't blame her, as such, but there was something in me that resented her, I just didn't really know what.

Anyway. All of a sudden we were down to four, and even then it felt like less. Kitty was barely ever around - now she had two sorrows to try and drown. Sophie still hadn't said a word, and so mostly it felt like it was just Alec and I. It was the loneliest I'd ever felt.

Now that I'd sat my final exams, I didn't have any formal lectures left. I think a lot of people were surprised when I'd signed up for the extra, post-exam classes, but they clearly didn't understand my need for distraction. There was no way in hell I was going back to my parents before I absolutely had to, and yet sitting around the house watching Kitty drink her life away seemed almost as bad. I started spending more time in the library, finally giving some of the books that Soph had recommended so many times a go. There was something calming about being surrounded by all the books and the silence.

It was about a week or so after the breakup that I was helping Alec make lunch. He'd been more and more withdrawn recently, spending more time in his room and less out here with us. One thing Louis' death had undoubtedly taught me was that I should appreciate any time I get with those I love, and so when he'd asked me to help him cook I'd jumped at the chance.

"So how's the play going?"

Alec shrugged. I missed the days where he seemed to care about his work.

"It's alright. We have tech this week, but it shouldn't be too hard. You've got your tickets right?"

"Course. Wouldn't miss it for the world."

"I've got a seat reserved for Kitty but…" Alec trailed off, but I knew where he was going with it. The play was an evening show, and I don't think she'd been sober after 6 o'clock in the last week.

"She in her room?"
"No, her studio."

I raised an eyebrow at Alec's answer and he nodded in agreement.

"I know, I was shocked too. But she left about ten minutes before you got in - I think she was already drinking. Just said she was going to the studio and was out the door before I could reply."

Something seemed wrong to me. Kit hadn't shown any interest in artwork since Louis' death, and so the fact that she'd all of a sudden run off to her studio seemed suspicious to me. The whole afternoon it dug at me, nerves clenching my stomach. It was when she didn't answer my phone call that I knew I had to go and check on her. I couldn't make the same mistake with Kitty that I'd made with Louis.

When I got to the studio, I could hear music blasting. I knocked a few times but as soon as I heard the smashing of glass I pushed on the door.

I was met with one of the most devastating sights ever. Kitty was sitting on the floor in the corner, head on her knees as she sobbed. There were countless vodka bottles on the floor next to her, and it made my heart sink to see how many of them were empty. The worst part by far, however, was the canvasses all over the floor. Some were smashed, huge cracks down the beautiful work. The ones which weren't cracked had bright red paint poured all over them, staining the stunning colours that had previously been there. It was heartbreaking to see. It had always been hard to see something so beautiful seem so broken and shattered - it was why it was hard to look at Kitty.

"Kit...what the hell did you do?" I whispered in horror, approaching her like a scared animal. She looked up at me, her face crumbling ever further.

"Kitty, speak to me," I ordered, trying to stay calm. It was only when she ignored me and took another swig from the bottle that I lost my patience.

"Fuck it. Kitty, this has gone too far. Drink yourself to death if you want, but get the hell out of the house. Leave."

As I stood to walk out, she looked up in shock, my words finally getting through to her.

"Wait, Seb, what? You're kicking me out?"

"I can't technically kick you out, Kit. You know that. But I am asking you to leave. Begging, even. If you're going to keep doing this to yourself, it can't happen here. I am not -"

I remember breaking off, my voice cracking painfully. I stared towards the ceiling, blinking away tears.

"I am not losing you too, Kit. I can't. It's not fair on me, or Alec, and it sure as hell isn't fair on Sophie. Fuck, Kitty, do you want her to have to find your body too?"

The look of horror on her face nearly made me feel guilty, but I couldn't bring myself to stop now I'd started.

"Seb, I wouldn't-"

"Oh wouldn't you? So are you telling me you've meant to do everything you've done these last few weeks? Get drunk and - by the looks of it, probably high - every night? Wake up more than once with your head in the toilet? Break Dani's heart? Wreck more than two years or your artwork? Fuck, Kitty, I don't know who you are anymore and it terrifies me. It's not fair, on any of us. So clean up or get the hell out because I won't watch you ruin yourself like this anymore."

I stood there, breathing heavily whilst waiting for an answer. Maybe if she'd stayed quiet that would have been the end of the argument, but she had to make one more comment, and I wasn't quite calm enough to take it.

"Seb, why are you so angry at me? Why are you so angry about me and Dani breaking-"

"BECAUSE YOU STILL GET YOUR CHANCE!" I screamed, and she jumped back in surprise. "You still get to know the love of your life, she's still here. Heck, she was in the same room as you! I don't get that luxury anymore. You have everything going for you and you blew it. I lost my chance and I can't watch you lose yours."

I didn't wait around to hear her reaction, storming out and enjoying the noise the door made as it slammed behind me.

Here's something I've come to realise over the years.

Of course, a lot of what I said that day was to do with Louis, that much was obvious. He shaped practically everything I said and did from that point on. But I also think a lot of what I said was to do with Sophie. I still couldn't look at her without thinking back to that hour where all she could do was scream. I'd felt protective of her ever since that day we spent smoking on the curb - she'd known she was barrelling towards darkness. Her words feel as though they're burned in me at all times.

"Oh, to be a cigarette, knowing I can cause so much damage without losing the person I need. Relying on others for light whilst hurtling towards the inevitable conclusion: burning out."

She'd always seemed softer and more gentle than the rest of us. She was strong, I know, but gave the impression of being easy to break. I still felt awful that it had to be her who found Louis. Maybe if I'd opened his door that night I could have changed that. I might not have been able to save him, but I could have saved her. It felt the same with Kitty - if she was dead set on spiralling downwards, there might not have been anything I could do. But I sure as hell could make sure she didn't do it anywhere near Sophie, not this time.

Thankfully my words had some effect on Kitty, because when I woke up the next morning, I found her pouring bottle after bottle down the sink. I didn't say anything, but I offered her a proud smile. That was all she needed.

I probably did go a bit too far that day, but I was scared. I loved Kitty so much, and I wholeheartedly believe that losing another friend would have destroyed me. Ever since Louis' death, I've put up walls, even now. Nobody has ever gotten as close to me, just in case. However, it was too late for everyone else at Northam. What could I say, they were under my skin.

CHAPTER TWELVE

"Life's but a walking shadow, a poor player

That struts and frets his hour upon the stage

And then is heard no more: it is a tale

Told by an idiot, full of sound and fury,

Signifying nothing."

- *Macbeth*

Kitty struggled those weeks after she poured the alcohol away, but she really tried. It was as though she had to build her confidence back up, and it was awful watching her fight with herself. She used to be so alive, bouncing into a room and having a kind word to say to everyone. Now it was as though she was waiting for permission to speak. I saw her watching Alec as he moved around the kitchen, a scared look on her face that only disappeared when one of us spoke to her. Whilst it hurt to have Sophie unable to speak, trying to adjust to a quiet Kitty was even harder.

It was a relief to have her back in the house at night, however. As much as I hated watching her so depressed, I found it easier to sleep knowing that instead of getting high in a stranger's kitchen, she was crying in her own room. Alec was in and out of the house almost as much as Kit had been, now that it was the week of the show. I was relying on the performance to distract us all from the ongoing nothing-ness that our lives had become.

The main problem was the same as before: Daniela. Kitty had been doing so well - as far as I knew, she hadn't touched a drop of alcohol since the studio incident - but we all knew she couldn't be properly happy without Dani. I don't think she was even capable of it. Losing someone you love - either through death or through your own mistakes - hurts. It feels like a gaping hole just filled with nothing. They say when you lose a limb it still has feeling, and I think it's the same with people. I could definitely feel Louis...or rather I could feel his absence. I don't know who had it worse; losing Louis and knowing there was nothing I could do, or Kitty losing Dani, knowing she could have changed matters.

It was an awful position to be in: judging who was in more pain.

Alec, Sophie and I tried our best to be there for Kitty, but I can't deny how hard it was. We did our best to stop drinking with her, but sometimes we needed it to cope too. On nights like that, the three of us ended up in my room, drinking wine from the bottle. We rarely spoke, and I always felt guilty about waiting until Kitty was asleep to do it. But it still felt nice to just sit there, in a comfortable silence.

Some nights we played board games, and often on those nights we'd ditch the wine and bring Kit in. We'd laugh and eat together, all sat cross-legged on the bed for most the night. In the tiny dorm, it was easy to pretend the outside world wasn't going on around us, easy to trick myself into thinking that Dani was just sleeping in her own house that night - that Louis had just turned in early.

As I was saying, we were relying on Alec's performance as a further distraction. The night before the show opened, Alec was more nervous that I'd ever seen him before. It seemed crazy to me - he was always perfect on stage. This was the performance that counted towards his final grade; something which made me nervous. Of course, Soph and I had already completed our exams, but Kitty and Alec relied on their work. We were still trying to find a way for Kitty to graduate at all - she'd lost two years of work in her meltdown at the studio. At the time, we were more focussed on making sure she made it to graduation.

We went back up the hill, that last night before the show. I really don't know when that place became where we went before big moments, but it definitely took on a new meaning. We sat on a blanket, eating grapes and running over his lines once more. There was one quote that stood out - *"I don't know why it is, but every time I reach out for something I want, I have to pull back because other people will suffer.*" It was one of Alec's lines, and it truly took on a new meaning. It reminded me of the kiss I still hadn't mentioned to anyone (though I'm sure Sophie knew). At the time it was all I wanted, and yet now I would swap it to have him alive, any day of the week.

The next day, the three of us took our seats, staring up at the stage. Despite everything, I still got the thrill of live theatre, the unpredictable nature of it all. As we edged down the aisle, I noticed Dani a few rows behind. Soph met my eye and it was almost as though we formed a mutual agreement to keep Kitty from noticing. She'd been doing so well, but we were all painfully aware that being reminded of what she'd lost could push her towards the edge.

The play started, and immediately I could see Alec was struggling. I'm sure it wasn't noticeable to the majority of the audience, but to someone who understood his behaviour as well as I did, it was as clear as day. His hands trembled so much during the first few scenes that he spent the rest of it with his hands in his pockets. He stuttered in a way that perhaps seemed in character for Chris Keller, but to Alec was inconceivable. At one point I remember glancing over and catching Kitty's eye, and she looked terrified. None of us had seen Alec like this, even in that first week since Louis' death. He'd always been the one who held it together more than the rest of us, and to see him fall apart was painful.

It wasn't until halfway through Act One that I remembered a line that was coming up, one which he'd always stumbled over in rehearsal. In our practices, he'd gritted his teeth and spat it out, but I dreaded having to watch him do it tonight, when he was so clearly falling apart. Watching the play unfold, I found I could barely concentrate on anything, hating that I had to watch him like this.

Finally the line before it was said, and my stomach clenched almost painfully. Please, God, let him get through this.

"Mother, please... Don't go through it all again, will you?" he announced, resting his arm on the fourth year playing Kate. She shook him off, and as he turned towards the audience, I could see tears in his eyes that weren't there beforehand.

"It's no good, it doesn't accomplish anything. I've been thinking, y'know…" he trailed off, and that was when something inside of him clearly broke. He put his hand to his mouth and sobbed, and I saw the rest of the cast turn to him in alarm. There was a brief moment of silence where everyone took a sudden intake of breath. He just stood there and sobbed, a hand over his face and another wrapped around his stomach. Eventually one of the other actors pulled him off stage, and the curtain fell. Chatter broke across the audience, and I stared at my feet in horror. My heart shattered for him.

He didn't come back on stage. His understudy stumbled through until the interval with a script in his hand and a makeshift costume, and it was almost painful to watch. As soon as the interval began, we ran from the auditorium, one of the crew wordlessly pointing towards Alec's dressing room. I was hesitant to go in, scared of what I would see.

He was crouched in the corner, head in his hand. Kitty went to him and wrapped her arms around him, letting him rest his head against her shoulder. Soph crouched in front of him, gripping his hands and pulling them away from his face. Before I could speak there was a knock on the door, and I turned to face it.

Dani was standing there, her eyeliner smudged with tears. I went to close the door on her, but she shoved her foot in before I could close it.

"He's my friend too, Seb. I'm as terrified as you. Let me in."

I hesitated, but ultimately I was always going to let her in. I could never say no to her.

"I fucked it all up. I'm never going to graduate," Alec muttered, in a voice that sounded like he had swallowed nails. Kitty was quick to offer words of comfort, but we all knew they were meaningless.

"Al, you did so well to get up there at all. Fuck, I could never have stood up there so soon after Louis," Dani told him, and Kitty was clearly biting back tears.

Even now, the look on Alec's face shatters me. He looked so helpless, like he'd lost any will to ever get back on that stage again. It was the same look I'd seen on Kitty's face when she'd smashed all of her art - a look that said 'even art can't save me now'.

"Alec, we're all so broken. None of us know what the hell we're doing. Kitty was trying to drink herself to death, Soph hasn't said a word in weeks, and ..." I trailed off. I didn't really know what to say about myself. My downward spiral was less obvious in many ways, and much less specific.

"We're going to get through this. We have to, right?" Kitty started, before pausing and glancing up at Dani. "We're all dying here, but we need to have some hope, some trust it's going to get better, or else what's the point?"

We all recognised the words, from the day of the breakup. Dani's words hadn't meant much at the time, all of us too lost in our own heartache, but now I was awake enough to fully understand them, I realised that Daniela was truly the smartest of us all.

The look she gave Kitty was so full of love that it nearly hurt to look at. I could see the inner turmoil in her gaze - how desperate she was to run to her, pull her into her arms and never let her go.

"I just...I miss him so much, you know? All the fucking time. He just left, he just went. He disappeared and...how are we supposed to deal with that? How can we just live with his absence?"

By the time Alec finished speaking, the whole room was in tears. Sophie's head was resting on Alec's knee, tears silently falling down her cheeks. He was hiccuping sadly, trying to slow down his sobs. It was Kitty who looked the most wrecked, her pale cheeks almost translucent. She glanced around the room, shaking her head.

"I'm so sorry, you guys. I'm...I'm so sorry," she sobbed, and this was what broke Dani. She was across the room in seconds, her arms around Kitty and her lips meeting hers. I wanted to glance away, but found I couldn't. The look of love on each of their faces almost gave me hope that maybe, just maybe, we could get through all of this.

"This isn't forgiveness, Kit, you still hurt me. You need to get better, because I swear to God, I can't do this again."
Kitty nodded frantically, her hair threading through Dani's as she littered kisses all over her hairline.

"I know, I promise, but...you're willing to try?" she asked, and the childish desperation in her voice made my heart ache. Dani thought about it for a second before giving her a soft smile, like a person watching the love of their life breaking apart.

"Yeah, KitKat, I am. I have hope, I have trust that it's going to get better, or else what's the point, right?"

The thing is, Alec never did finish the speech on stage. He'd broken down before he'd properly reached the hardest part; he knew it was coming and it clearly broke him. I'm sure nobody else knew the quote was unfinished, but I had spent so many evenings running lines with Alec that I was practically word perfect.

I've never re-read All My Sons, knowing it would be too painful, too tainted with memories of that awful evening. When writing this, however, I searched for the script, and was reminded of just why it was so difficult for Alec to get through it. I think it's pretty self explanatory, considering the circumstances.

"Mother, please... Don't go through it all again, will you? It's no good, it doesn't accomplish anything. I've been thinking, y'know? ...maybe we ought to put our minds to forgetting him?"

We never could get around to forgetting him. It was an impossible task, and even the thought of doing so was enough to move Alec to tears.

I understood how he felt.

CHAPTER THIRTEEN

"Self-love, my liege, is not so vile a sin, as self-neglecting."

- *Henry V*

Somehow, the term began to end. It shouldn't have been a surprise; after all, we'd all sat our final exams and projects, and therefore the end of term was inevitable. But it still felt wrong to be completing the year at Northam so soon.

There was one last event before the year ended; the end of term ball. It was somewhat a tradition of the school, apparently, but after everything that had happened I was reluctant to go at all. It felt wrong to dress up and celebrate surviving the year. It felt a bit like a kick in the teeth, I suppose.

I kept these issues to myself of course. Kitty was excited, and now that she was capable of smiling I was doing everything in my power to keep it that way. Dani hadn't slipped back into the group seamlessly, and it was clear she wanted to protect herself. Every time she saw Kitty drink water in place of wine, though, I could feel a wall or two coming town. I understood her need to adjust slowly, but I couldn't deny that it made me unreasonably happy to have her back. Maybe it was because Kitty was so happy - my joy always did rely on others.

Alec and I went suit shopping in town, and it felt nice to do something so mundane.

"Ah, you are both handsome boys! Let's find you a suit to make your girlfriends swoon, yes?" The tailor asked, and I fought back the urge to elbow Alec as he snorted. We both knew what that was in reference to, even if neither of us had ever addressed it. I was, of course, going to the ball alone, but I didn't even mind. I'd initially considered going with Sophie - strictly as friends, of course - but I'd overheard Kitty telling Dani that someone had already asked her. I was intrigued to meet this mystery man, and I already felt a protective instinct similar to the way a brother would act. Over the last few months I'd become somewhat of a bodyguard for Sophie, defending her when it felt like she couldn't.

Alec was going with a girl from his drama class - Valentina, I think her name was. At the time it didn't even occur to me that I would be the only one going alone.

I ended up picking out a dark green suit, one which was plain but, according to Alec at least, "bought out the colour in my eyes." I wasn't aware my brown eyes could even be seen properly behind my glasses, but I knew better than to argue with Alec over fashion. He picked out a black suit with gold leaves sewn right down the left arm, and it was almost comforting to see him choose something so dramatic it reminded me of old Alec. The girls had insisted that we didn't see their outfits until the day of the ball, and so Alec spent the whole day fretting that we would clash with them in photographs.

It made my heart hurt to think about being photographed by anyone but Louis.

I realise now that their excitement about the ball was purely a distraction from the fear of graduating, but at the time it just seemed like we were recovering. The girls spent the day of the ball running around in dressing gowns and their hair in straighteners, whilst Alec and I watched the chaos unfold. It felt so normal, and I seized it with both hands.

I remember how everyone looked in such vivid detail that it surprises me. It's just a memory which, no matter what, can't seem to fade. Sophie was wearing a pale blue dress, her long skirt swirling around her as she walked. Her blond hair was mostly pinned up in her typical plaits, twisted across her head with loose curls falling against her shoulders. She looked stunning, and the second I saw her I remembered that day during the Ancient Greek party, with the gold glitter lighting up her eyes. Most importantly, she looked truly happy. She was smiling as she was pulled into photographs with us all, and that was where the true beauty lay.

Her date to the dance was a student from her course - Teddy. I'd seen him around campus but this was the first time I'd ever spoken to him, and within seconds I knew he was perfect for Soph. He seemed taken aback with how beautiful she looked, but the most notable thing was he never asked her questions she would have to answer. I don't know how long they'd known each other before the ball, but that evening he never once put her in the uncomfortable position of having to look on helplessly. He didn't seem to blink at her silence, and she seemed truly at ease with him. Even my brotherly instincts couldn't seem to fault him.

Kitty had been nervous about the upcoming ball, still not quite sure where she stood with Dani. I don't know why she ever worried - Dani was unable to stay away for too long. It was weird to see Kit in a dress, so used to seeing her in oversized hoodies and paint-stained dungarees. That being said, she looked stunning. Of course she did; I don't think Kitty was capable of looking anything but beautiful. Her dress was a deep scarlet colour which made her hair seem even darker than normal, her short bob falling in soft curls just touching her shoulder. The dress was low cut with a slit up the side, and we all took great amusement in watching Dani cough on her prosecco when Kitty walked in. In just the same way as seeing Sophie so happy made her even prettier, seeing Kit so in love made her even more stunning.

Daniela wore a suit, naturally, and I truly believe she pulled it off better than I did. It was a black velvet suit, the blazer jacket covering up a lacy cami top, made of a red material that perfectly matched Kitty's dress. The sleeves were rolled up to reveal her tattoos, and she seemed so comfortable in her outfit it was almost difficult to imagine her wearing anything else.

I couldn't help but let my mind wander to what Louis would have worn, had he attended. I could see him wearing a dark blue suit, perhaps, one which highlighted his blond curls. I hope he wouldn't do anything with his hair; Alec had his slicked back, but I couldn't picture Louis without the long curls obscuring his eyes.

All of this was futile, but my mind can't help where it goes sometimes.

The ball itself was being held in a fancy hotel in town, and the entire place was decorated with fairy lights. It was stunning, and I remember countless photographs being taken by practically everyone. I wasn't one for dancing, so I spent a lot of the evening standing off to one side, simply enjoying the music. We were all handed a glass of prosecco upon entrance, and I could almost feel Dani's elation when Kitty turned it down with ease. She pulled Kit onto the dancefloor, and I don't think they left it all night. I can't remember which song it was exactly - some slow song played with a soft guitar backing - but I watched Dani pull her into her arms and whisper into Kitty's ear, and I was filled with contentment. The two of them looked so happy that I could almost hope that maybe we would make it after all.

We need to have some hope, some trust it's going to get better, or else what's the point?

I don't think I could pinpoint an actual moment during the night where I went from passive boredom to feeling an almost overwhelming sentiment of sadness. I slipped outside for a cigarette, and on my way out I caught Sophie's eye. She raised an eyebrow, and even without words I could tell she was offering to come out with me. I shook my head - she seemed so happy with Teddy, and I would never take her away from that.

I stood outside on the balcony, inhaling the smoke deeply and trying to focus more on the way it looked upon hitting the cold air, and less on the spirally feeling that I was losing them all. I didn't know what the end of term would bring, but I knew enough to be wary of change. The street the balcony was looking over seemed familiar, and it didn't take me long to realise it was from Louis' photos. They were the ones that had caused all of this, the ones which the man had been in.

I made no attempt to slow the tears falling, merely staring up at the sky and waiting. It was nice, out on the balcony. It wasn't too cold, and whilst the quiet was nice, you could still hear the music from inside. It felt a little less lonely that way, like I was still connected with reality.

"Got a light?"

Alec stirred me from my thoughts, reaching for the cigarette in my hand. He breathed in deeply, his eyes closed, and I could see him relaxing with every breath. I noticed with a smirk that his lips were slightly stained with red, something which I wasted no time in pointing out.

"Mmm, it's a good colour on me, huh? I don't know, she's nice. She's not from Northam, which feels good. Outsider perspective, less baggage." I nodded, tugging at his arm before he handed my cigarette back to me.

"Plus she's smoking hot, that helps too," he added, and I couldn't stop myself from rolling my eyes.

"What do you think of Teddy?"

Alec hummed, thinking it over.

"He seems kind of perfect for her. He's got the soft literature vibe down, at least. I don't know, I always thought you'd end up with her, if I'm being honest."

This surprised me - I always thought nobody had noticed the initial awkwardness between me and Soph.

"Yeah, that was before we all realised, of course," he added, and I couldn't help but sigh. I'd forgotten Alec knew - after all, it was him who had made the Achilles and Patroclus reference.

"I'm happy for her. She deserves to be happy," I replied, glancing over my shoulder at where she was dancing.

"Yeah. They're letting me make up part of my final grade, by the way. They still have to count the All My Sons performance, but it's being moved to 60% instead of 80. It means they can count some of my Shakespeare work, maybe the Present Laughter one too - hopefully it'll get my grade up enough to graduate, at least."

"That's great! If they're including any of your other performances then you're sorted. You're the best actor I know." I meant it. Until that day, I'd never seen Alec so much as falter when performing, and I hoped I never would again.

"Any idea what Kitty's planning to do? She has time right?" Alec sounded worried as he asked, but still said in a tone that suggested he didn't want anyone to know how concerned he was. All of us were trying to deny the situation she was in, but that could only go on for so long.

"Yeah, she appealed - I think they're giving her an extension until the end of the holiday instead of the start, hopefully she can at the very least create a final piece."

We stood out on the balcony in silence, and I remember debating whether to mention which street we were on. I kept forgetting that the others didn't really have any idea why Louis had started his downward spiral back before christmas, and yet I couldn't bring myself to tell any of them. It made me feel a little special, having this secret connection to him.

"Look, I'm going to head home, I'm not really feeling this tonight, you know?" I announced suddenly, feeling the urge to be back at home. I always struggled with being in situations where you were supposed to be happy. Alec frowned and tried his best to convince me to stay, but ultimately I pushed him back towards Valentina and made me quick exit. As I walked back through the town towards Northam, I couldn't help but stand outside the bakery from Louis' photos, staring up at the window. For the first time ever I found myself angry that I didn't have answers, found myself understanding why Louis lost hope when answers became impossible.

I took the long route again back up to Northam, which was, in hindsight, a stupid idea. It was past midnight by the time I could see Northam in the distance, and I ended up using my phone as a light, unable to see much in the dark. Back home, it was impossible to see the stars at night, what with all the pollution. Out here though, in the middle of the woods, it was easy to see them clearly.

Maybe if I'd not been looking up at the stars I would have noticed that part of the path had collapsed into the valley. My body was falling before I'd even registered what was happening, and I stayed conscious just long enough to hear the sickening crack my arm made upon impact.

As everything faded black, I could only think about one thing.

Let them bury my bones with his.

CHAPTER FOURTEEN

"One fire burns out another's burning, One pain is lessen'd by another's anguish."

- *Romeo And Juliet*

I lay in that ditch until the sun began to rise. I remember feeling the blood trickling down the side of my face - the first clue that I'd hit my head. The second was the unbearable waves of dizziness I had to fight off every time I tried to move.

My arm lay under me, and it felt almost as if it was on fire. It burned from the wrist to the shoulder, and even the thought of moving it made me sick.

I remember being terrified. I don't think I'd ever been so scared. It felt like I was trapped, unable to move and never knowing when - or even, if - someone would get help. I had to reconcile with the idea of never seeing Northam again. Never being able to walk up those stone stairs and see the building peeking through the trees. Never be able to walk up to Louis' hill, look over campus or go to the theatre again.

Never hear Kitty's laugh again. I couldn't cope with the reality that, if nobody could find me, I would never get to see her and Dani achieve the happiness they deserved. Never see Alec yell Shakespeare from a stage, never see him stand on the sofa and smile so wide that I couldn't help but smile too. I wouldn't be able to hug Sophie again, never see her soft smile, never watch her plait her hair obsessively.

I think I had some form of breakdown, laying in the dirt and desperately trying to stay awake.

I was never going to see Louis again. I'd known this, of course, I'd known it for months. I knew I wouldn't hear his laugh again, I knew I would never see the way his face lit up when he saw something he needed to photograph.

I needed to survive. I needed to find some way to climb out, or to fetch help. I couldn't allow this to be the end - Sophie, Kitty, Alec and Dani deserved better than that. Nobody should ever have to lose a friend - and they definitely shouldn't have to lose two. I don't know when my survival began to rest on the happiness of others, but it was what got me through the night.

I can't remember much about how I managed to sit up, other than the excruciating pain. I held my arm against my chest, crying out in pain every time I moved it. My phone had survived the fall, and when I saw that it still had battery I cried in relief. It was just past five, and it was a sickening realisation that I'd been laying here in the cold for five hours. I couldn't quite be sure if I was shivering from the cold, the pain, or from the shock, but I had a hard time unlocking my phone.

I called Kitty, hoping she would be the only sober one. I managed to give her a garbled message, my vision fading the more I spoke. I remember the phone slipping from my grasp as soon as I gave her my location - vaguely hearing her call my name.

Please, God, let them find me.

*

I woke up in hospital, and before I even opened my eyes I could feel someone gripping my hand. My brain felt foggy - I'd had copious amounts of anaesthesia pumped into my body, I later realised - and it took a few tries to open my eyes.

When I did, everything was blurry. I don't know whether that was through the drugs, the head injury, or the fact I wasn't wearing my glasses. I slowly turned my head, seeing the room swirl around me.

I could see blond hair and blue eyes staring at me through the fog, their hand tugging on mine. I squeezed back, squinting as I tried to make my eyes focus. The smile they gave me was beautiful, and I felt a sense of calm fill me.

"Louis," I whispered, before falling back to sleep.

When I woke again, I glanced over and saw Sophie holding my hand, fast asleep. Alec was laying on the sofa, and Daniela was at the end of the bed, curled around my feet.

"Seb, thank God." Kitty was suddenly leaning over me, her face somehow both terrified and relieved. She was in a hoodie and jeans, but her hair and makeup were still the same as the night before.

"Hi, you found me," I whispered happily, still fighting with the effects of the drugs. She ran a hand through my hair, wincing as she ran her finger over the stitches along my hairline.

"Yeah angel, we found you. Your arm was broken in three places, they operated on it whilst you were out. You also have a pretty nasty cut along your head. Fuck, Seb. What were you thinking?"

"I wasn't. I just wanted a walk, I got distracted by the stars. He always loved the stars, you know? He had posters of constellations up around his room. I just wanted to look at them," I muttered, watching her sleepily.

"Yeah, I know Seb. But next time, just don't do it in the middle of your night on your own, okay?"

I nodded again, letting my eyes close again.

It took four days, but I was finally allowed to go home. I hated staying in the hospital - the others came as much as they could, but at the end of the day they would have to leave, and I'd be left alone. Soph had bought books for me, but the painkillers were so strong that I found it hard to focus on anything I read.

Alec drove me home, helping me up the stairs. Even after a few days, my movements were sluggish, and for the rest of the week I stayed mostly in my room, only ever shuffling to and from the bathroom. Kitty had stayed for a day or so, but as soon as I found out she was skipping studio time to stay with me, I forced her out of the room.

My arm began to heal, of course, and yet I still found the cast tiresome. It was quite an adjustment, getting used to having to operate with only one arm. On one of the first nights back, Kitty sat with my arm in her lap for nearly three hours, delicately painting the cast with a Starry Night scene. It was magical to see, watching her stick her tongue out in concentration as she painted. It was a shame when it had to be cut off and replaced at my check up the next week.

Another thing I'd noticed since that night was a sudden dislike of the dark. I wouldn't say I was scared of it, necessarily, but I was finding it hard to switch off. I'd try to sleep, but the same thoughts from the bottom of the valley would come flooding back. I found myself thinking about all the things, all the people I would lose if I'd died down there, and it made it hard to ever relax. I knew I was heading towards a crash, but I just found it easier to spend the nights reading or watching old films rather than attempt to sleep. It wasn't like I needed an abundance of energy anyhow - my days were spent laying in bed or on the sofa, rarely even bothering to get dressed.

I didn't attend any of the extra classes I'd signed up for, knowing they didn't count for anything anyway.

Thinking about it now, I think this was my 'Louis breakdown'. We'd all had one - mine was just less obvious. Kitty's was alcohol fuelled, Alec's was the play, of course. It seemed fitting - both Kitty and Alec's breakdowns were loud and messy, mine and Sophie's were silent and private. It summed us up as people, I suppose.

On one of the days whilst I was recovering, I found myself alone in the house. I wandered past everyone's doors but realised they must have all gone out, so padded through into the kitchen. I spent an hour or so playing with Ariel, dangling a shoelace in front of her and watching her bat at it with her tiny paws. The only time I bothered to get up was to refill her water bowl, but it still made me more energised, enjoying doing something so light and carefree.

"Well isn't that a cute sight," Dani announced, leaning down to scratch Ariel's fur before doing the same to me.

"Get off. Where's everyone else?"

"Alec is freaking out, so they went to get chocolate. Grades come out in about ten minutes - remember?"

I hadn't.

In fact, I'd forgotten about my exams practically as soon as I sat them. This year had been so eventful, so dramatic, that the thought of caring about something so mundane as exams seemed ridiculous. That was a problem normal people had, not me.

I had to care though. What was the point if I didn't? I knew, logically, that they were important, even if my brain didn't seem to be registering that.

I didn't feel I needed to worry about any of us. Out of the four of us getting our results - Kitty's extension was allowing her another month into the holidays - nobody was going to fail, I was sure of it. Now that Alec's other performances had been counted, I was sure he'd make the 60 marks needed to pass. Dani had never gotten under 75, and Soph was bound to do more than enough; she'd taken the exams in her stride. Sophie was the kind of person who considered anything below 80 a failure, despite being the first person to celebrate anyone else's grades, no matter how low. She'd never give herself a break, but she never needed to - she always did well.

When the emails came through, I felt everyone take a nervous breath.

Alec whooped, breaking into the chocolate bar he'd bought in celebration.

"72! Considering I didn't reach Act One in my final play, I'll take that."

We all congratulated him, before turning to Daniela. She was blushing happily, and Kitty was laughing.

"God, you're such a nerd. 83. Ridiculous."

Nobody was surprised - Dani was a hurricane when it came to her music. I'd never seen someone who found her craft so easy, it came so naturally to her.

"Seb?"

I grinned.
"79."

Everyone congratulated me, and I let out a breath I didn't know I was holding. As much as I said I didn't care, I was still dictated by the fear of failure. Whilst it wasn't as high as it could be, given the circumstances I was more than happy.

And then I looked at Sophie.

She was staring at her hands, biting her lip. I glanced at Kitty nervously, before softly calling Soph's name.

"Soph? How did you do?"

She shook her head slowly, and I was reminded of the high standard she held herself to. Alec was clearly thinking the same thing, nudging her lightly.

"Come on Soph, you'd be upset with 95. Bet you smashed it."

She sighed, looking up at us all before handing me the phone.

61.

She'd passed, just about. I wouldn't have even blinked - after the hell she'd been through it was impressive she'd turned up to the exam. But I knew this wouldn't comfort Sophie. I wordlessly handed the phone to the others, who clearly had more hope than me.

"Sophie, look at me. Eyes up here," Dani ordered, taking her hand. When Sophie did what she was told, Daniela raised her eyebrows and gave her a stern look.

"You did well. You did so well. I know you're disappointed, and that's okay, but we're so proud of you. Right guys?"

"Absolutely. Heck, you didn't get any special considerations unlike Alec and I. You did well Soph, don't beat yourself up."

Sophie nodded at Kitty before looking at me, throwing me a helpless look.

"I'm so proud of you, and so is Louis," I muttered, knowing this would cause a ripple in the room. They all winced, but it was what Sophie needed to hear. She nodded again, smiling at me gratefully.

"And hey! We all get to graduate!" Alec announced, trying his best to lighten the mood.

That night truly showed just how much everything had changed. Pre-Louis, we would have thrown a themed party, putting special detail into decorations and costumes, and gotten exceedingly drunk. Instead, our celebration was private and understated. It was just the five of us, and all we did was drink wine, eat chocolate and listen to music. I don't think we had it in us to properly celebrate, and this relaxed evening suited us just fine. I danced as much as I could with only one arm, and it made me feel nearly human.

I'll say it now - I was terrified of the holidays. I didn't know what they would bring, and I didn't want to leave Northam. It didn't feel as though I knew how to exist outside of those walls anymore.

At some point that night, I decided I needed to try and get some answers. I couldn't leave without at least trying to find something out about the man in the photos. I wasn't like Louis - I didn't need all the answers, I just needed to know something, anything.

CHAPTER FIFTEEN

"And since you know you cannot see yourself,

so well as by reflection, I, your glass,

will modestly discover to yourself,

that of yourself which you yet know not of."

- *Julius Caesar*

The next day, I made up some excuse about having a check-up on my arm, and headed into town. I don't know why I didn't want to tell them, but it still felt like something I should keep to myself. I did, at the very least, stick to the main paths this time.

The town by the school was an old mining town, all stone buildings and small lanes. It felt a little like stepping into the past, like the living museums my school used to take the history classes to when I was young. It was the sort of town where everyone knew everyone, and this was what I was hoping for.

I'd luckily got a copy of one of Louis' photos with him in. I don't think I'd even be here if I didn't; there was no way I was going into Louis' room to find another one. A cleaner had been sent in by the university to make sure there was no food in there, but we'd been reluctant to go anywhere near the room.

My first stop was the bakery, as that was the shop in the background of Louis' photo. There was a large oak tree in front of it, and so Alec loved photographing it throughout the year, enjoying capturing the seasons. We always loved when Alec photographed it; he always bought cakes back for us. The woman said she recognised him, but didn't know his name. I was about to leave when she called me back, suggesting I asked at the pharmacy. On the walk over I couldn't help but clench my fists in nervousness. I desperately wanted to find some answers, even if it was something basic.

When I handed the photo to the woman behind the counter, she frowned.

"Yes, that's Archie. He lived in the cottage down on Rose Hill road, the one on the corner. His wife Dee still lives there. He came here regularly, he was a loyal customer. We all miss him around here."

I nodded and thanked her, but before I could leave she called after me.

"What's this about? It's just, another boy was in here a while back, asking after Archie. About your age. I told him the same thing I told you."

I stumbled through an answer, not wanting to get into it here.

I found the cottage, and it made me even more confident in my assurance that there was no darker motive behind his presence in Louis' photos. It seemed like your average cottage, with flower pots along the path and an old wooden door. It took me a while to get up the courage to knock, but ultimately I knew I couldn't leave Northam without getting some answers. It felt comforting to know Louis too had stood here, probably just as nervous as me.

When I finally knocked, a woman appeared at the door. She was perhaps in her mid-40s, hands covered in dough.

"Um, hello ma'am. I'm Sebastian Blackwood, I was wondering if I could ask you a few questions about your husband?"

She sighed in a tone that suggested deep grief. It was a sound I'd become deeply accustomed to.

She let me in, telling me to sit at the kitchen table as she continued to bake her bread.

"You know, you're the second person to come around asking about Archie. A boy came around about a week or two after his death. Are you with him?"

What a question.

"Um, yes. Sort of. He was my friend...he passed away earlier this year. He was doing a project on people in the town, and your husband was the only one unfinished. I was just wondering if you could tell me what you told my friend? I'll take anything you've got."

Dee thought for a moment, and I almost considered giving up and leaving. Who was I to make a poor woman talk through her grief? Eventually she answered though, and sat down opposite me.

"I'm sorry to hear about your friend, he seemed like a nice boy. I'm not sure I remember much about what I told him, but I can try my best."

I reassured her that anything she had would be helpful, and she nodded again.

"Okay then. Well...I met Archie at school. We both went to the university just outside of the town. I studied mechanics whilst he studied the Classics. Greek, Latin, you know. He was always a part of this special little group, they all lived up on that hill together. North-something. Northridge?"

I sat forward in my seat. "He went to Northam?"

"Yes, Northam, that was it. He was always up there, all mysterious and elite. It was only when we left school that we actually got to know each other. At the time, he was just pretentious. We got together right after he broke up with his girlfriend - a Northam girl, I think. It was a long time ago."

I couldn't wrap my head around the fact that he went to Northam - had Louis known this? How had someone from Northam ended in this little cottage? From the sounds of it, he'd been just like us.

"After we left school, he gave up on most of the classic nonsense, took a job working in the shop down the road and stayed there for most his life. I can't say he was perfect - he put me through hell with his drinking - but we had a good life together."

"His drinking?" I was almost scared to ask, but I knew I would regret it if I didn't.

"God, yes. It's what killed him," she said somberely. "I think it probably started when we were still young, and he just never really kicked the habit. Archie...he wasn't a happy man. I think he always wanted more, you know? We always said he was destined for more, but that's just not how the world works any more."

I could hear the meaning behind her words - there was no room for artists anymore.

It was only when I was saying my goodbyes and thanking her for her time that I noticed a photo behind her on the fireplace. It was Archie - much younger than in any of Louis' photos - with his arms around two friends. In normal circumstances, this would hardly be significant, after all - it was his home. Of course photos of him would be on the fireplace.

The bit that got me, however, was the people he had his arms around.

Louis' parents.

I blinked a few times, pulling myself back into the room. Dee was standing near the door, watching as I just stared behind her. Even though I had no idea where my mind was going with this, I had one overwhelming thought: if i leave this house, I will never get any form of answer.

"Uh, could I...um...could I use your bathroom?" I stumbled over my words, my mouth making the excuse before my brain could really catch up. She nodded and pointed me upstairs, and I headed straight towards a room I knew wasn't the bathroom.

I remember my heart pounding as I edged into the room, hardly daring to turn on the light. Trying to stay as quiet as I could, I went straight to the chest of drawers, wincing as the old wood squeaked slightly. When this drawer revealed nothing but clothes, I turned towards the desk. As I flicked through some paperwork, I remember feeling thoroughly sick with myself. This could all be nothing - maybe they just went to Northam together. Who was I to look through a dead man's desk, with his widow just downstairs? Just as I was about to give up and go back down, I noticed a photo album. It was tucked behind some other files - the sort of thing which, to a sane person would just seem normal but in my heightened, panicked, and probably paranoid state, seemed hidden.

When I opened it, I knew straight away that I was right to do so. It felt like the numbness that had taken over me these last few weeks was suddenly melting away and I was feeling everything at once. Multiple Louis' stared back at me - most from a long distance. It terrified me. I recognised some of them - photos posted on the school's websites, one from the advert for his exhibition, another from his memorial service. Most of them, however, were blurry and grainy, clearly taken from across roads. In ones where other people had clearly been with him, the photo had been cut so it was simply Louis in shot.

I remember the resounding thought in my mind: God, I should have believed him.

Replacing the photo album and shutting the desk drawer, I walked into the bathroom, flushed the toilet, ran the tap for a few seconds and headed back downstairs. The entire time I was leaving the house, my heart was pounding.

It was only when I'd turned the corner that I pulled out the photo I'd taken from the desk. It was just one of Archie, sitting in his kitchen. I hoped that the mundane nature of the photo would mean Dee wouldn't notice it was missing, it was why I didn't risk taking all of the others. I had no doubt that I could remember his face perfectly, but the photograph wasn't for me. I knew I needed answers, and I would only get them from Louis' parents.

I couldn't bring myself to go straight home, needing to process everything she'd said. I sat on a wall, wincing against the ache in my arm. It wasn't even just the Louis connection - it was everything. Archie's life drew some dangerous parallels.

It seemed ridiculous to me that someone from Northam, someone who seemed to be just as obsessed with learning and the arts as we were, would end up in a small town, depressed and dissatisfied. I know it seemed pretentious, but we'd always been told we were destined for better things. I didn't know what would happen in the future, but I could exclusively see success for my friends. I never doubted that they would turn into the sort of people I would brag about knowing, the sort of people who everyone would look up to. In my naivety, I'd imagined this was always the case for people at Northam. It wasn't that I saw it as a free pass, necessarily - we all worked exceptionally hard - but it just seemed an accepted fact: we were supposed to do something great, even me. I'd destined myself to a life recording the achievements of great people without necessarily being one - but that was fine. Someone needed to live to tell their story, and that was my role in life.

Alec was meant to go out and move people to tears with his work, he was meant to transport people away from reality in a way that could only be described as magical. Kitty was meant to put beauty into the world, making sure that life was captured through the incredible way she saw things. Soph was meant to not just read and interpret the words of others, but to write her own, create her own poetry. Daniela's music was meant to make people feel, make people just..happy. The same way she made Kitty happy.

I couldn't reconcile with the fact that not only did I see us in the young version of Archie, I could see us in the older him too. He'd lost the inspiration that had originally governed him, and he'd turned to alcohol; the comparison to Kitty was undeniable. I knew she had been doing so much better recently, but the threat of relapse was always there. Both Kitty and Alec had destroyed part of their art because of how scared and lost they were.

I definitely understood what she'd meant when she said he was dissatisfied with life. I'd spent the weeks since my accident walking around in a bit of a daze. They say a near death experience was meant to wake you up, but it just made me want to go to sleep.

Maybe by considering the finality of my own death I was fully made aware of the finality of his.

I didn't get all of the answers I wanted, but I got what I needed. I saw the reality of what my life was barrelling towards, and it pushed me to change. I didn't want to end up like him. I didn't want any of us to end up like him. I couldn't let myself slip away into depression or alcoholism, and seeing Archie - who had, in so many ways, been just like us - had been a stark wake up call.

When I arrived back at Northam, it was as though I was seeing everyone for the first time in weeks. They were all their own people, with their own lives, and because of the hole I'd been in since my accident, I'd lost sight of this. I'd been walking through life almost as though I wasn't real, and everything was merely a fictitious creation. It was only when I imagined Archie - who, by the sounds of it, had spent his whole life in this dark cloud of dissatisfaction - that I realised I had to break out of it as quickly as I could.

I hugged Sophie for the longest time, and even without saying anything it almost felt as though she was fixing everything. I got Kitty to repaint my new cast - this time she decorated it like The Great Wave off Kanagawa. The beaming grin she gave me when I finally acknowledged her properly for the first time in weeks allowed me to breath just a little easier.

I'd neglected my friends over the weeks since the accident, and that's just a fact. I'd been so wrapped up in my own shroud of despair that I hadn't wanted it to hurt anyone else, so I just contained myself to my room. I was determined to avoid ending up like Archie, and if this was the first step in doing so, I was going to make it.

That night, as I laid in bed, I knew I had to visit Louis' parents. I wouldn't be able to visit until the end of term, but I could wait.

CHAPTER SIXTEEN

"Doubt thou the stars are fire;

Doubt that the sun doth move;

Doubt truth to be a liar;

But never doubt I love."

    -   Hamlet

There is one last day to tell you about before the term ended.

That last week, there was the underlying tension - nobody wanted to leave. This place had held an unbelievable and insurmountable amount of grief and heartache, but it had also been our home. Nowhere else had I ever felt such love. Hell, I learnt what family meant at Northam. The idea of leaving meant stepping outside this bubble we'd created for ourselves, and having to live life outside of here. It seemed a task that was just slightly too difficult, and so we tried our best to ignore it.

This was a difficult task in itself; the passage of time seemed to be taunting us. Everything seemed to be the last of something - the last time we cooked dinner together, the last trip into town, the last lecture. It was as though, despite the effort we put into making everything normal, it was all tainted with an underlying sense of sadness.

It was stupid, looking back on it. Leaving Northam didn't necessarily mean we had to lose touch - we largely did, sadly, but that didn't always have to be the case. Yet, every time we saw another with a suitcase or saw someone packing their plates away instead of simply leaving them in the drawer, it felt like a sharp pain in my stomach.

When I first moved in, I described my room as impersonal and empty. This had undoubtedly changed over my time there. Instead of the blank walls, they now had large displays of photographs and paper I'd collected over the years. Very little of it is on display in my house now, but I think I can vaguely remember most of it. There were little postcards that Kitty had painted us for our birthdays - mine was cartoon drawings of me as different historical figures, and a little copy of her edition of Liberty Leading The People. It still stung to think of that painting; it truly hurt to think of it on the floor of the studio, slashed through with bright red paint. There were tickets from various museum trips, a few photos of Louis' that didn't make the exhibition. I think there were some scribbles of Dani's lyrics, some of Sophie's favourite quotes that she'd written out in ink. It felt like a home, something that was lived in rather than the empty hotel-style room I'd first moved into.

There was another thing we would be leaving behind - Louis' room. It had been left untouched, none of us brave enough to step inside. The door had remained firmly closed, and sometimes it felt as though "do not enter" tape should have been stuck across.

Somehow we reached the last night at Northam, and it felt a little like I was going to fall apart if I didn't smile. We all seemed to be thinking the same thing, and so as we blasted Dani's music and ate the pizza we'd ordered sat on the floor, we laughed louder than we had for a long while. Kitty told stories we'd all heard a hundred times before, and yet we enjoyed them just as much as if it had been the first. Alec started a Shakespeare contest which dissolved into Kit and I making up quotes, unsure how to keep this game going without Sophie's expertise.

Soph wandered off half way through dinner, and we all shared a sympathetic look. She must be hurting just as much as we all were, but without the loud and manic outlet, she couldn't distract herself.

When I left the kitchen to fetch a towel following Alec's wine accident during a particularly dramatic rendition of Lady Macbeth's soliloquy, I noticed something was different. In a cruel twist of irony, almost as if the universe was mocking me, I noticed that Louis' door was open.

Of course I noticed the door this time.

I pushed it open cautiously, afraid of the memories it would cause. Sophie was sitting just inside the door, kneeling down. She'd clearly looked in the top drawer of his desk, where I knew he kept all of his photos. She was surrounded by thousands of them, barely an inch of carpet visible. She was gripping one of the ones from that day on the steps, one of the ones of all of us. When she looked up at me, silent tears were falling down her face and she looked wrecked. It broke me. Without saying a word, I left the room and when I returned, they all followed me. We stood in the doorway and it felt eerily familiar. It took me straight back to the day all those months ago, where we stood in this exact doorway and our world fell apart a little.

"God...he photographed everything," Kitty whispered, sitting next to Soph and picking up a pile nearest her. She was right, our whole lives at Northam had been documented. I glanced up at Alec, and I could tell just how hard he was trying to stay strong, his jaw set firmly. He blinked a few times before nodding, and picking up the ones at his feet.

"Let's take them in the kitchen, we can sort through them there."

I can't remember how many trips it took for us to carry the literal thousands of photos through to the kitchen, but I remember it felt like hundreds. Every time I entered his room, it got a little easier to breath.

It felt fitting that our last night should be spent with Louis - as close as we could get, at least. Early in the night, we realised we couldn't keep the photographs, not all of them. The sheer number was overwhelming, but it also hurt too much. We didn't want to track our lives through the eyes of our dead friend. That's no way to live.

The options, as we saw it, were as follows. We could throw them away, we could sell them, or we could leave them at Northam. The first seemed too cruel, the second too commercial. We considered leaving them here, but we couldn't risk someone finding them. These were our entire lives, and we didn't want someone looking through them.

It was Dani, I think, who suggested we burn them. I know it sounds cruel, but it was more of a celebration than anything else. We each went through a chose a couple we wanted to keep, and the rest we took up to the hill.

It would have been the perfect opportunity to tell the others about the man in the photos. He was in so many from the town photo set, and every time I saw him I heard his wife's subtle warning: there was no room for artists anymore. I wouldn't let that be true.

Dani's two photos were both from the 1940s party. One was a group shot, all of us gathered around the sofa. We're all grinning at Louis behind the camera, and Alec is reaching out, beckoning him. The second is one of just her and Kitty, dancing in the garden. It's almost fictionally perfect, the fairy lights framing them both. Dani has her arms wrapped around Kit, who is leaning back, arms wide. I often struggled to understand what Louis found in a lot of his photos - he saw beauty in such normal things - but in this case, it was plain to see. It looked so beautiful it almost hurt to look at.

Kitty's photos were similar, also choosing one of us all - this time it was one of the ones from that photoshoot on the stairs, the one where nobody was looking at the camera; a true candid. I'd never seen the second photo before - it was of Kitty and Dani in her studio, apparently taken before I'd even arrived at Northam. Neither were facing the camera; Kitty was sitting at an easel painting, and Dani was standing behind her, her arms around her with her chin resting on Kitty's shoulder. I don't know what was more beautiful - how happy they were, or the artwork itself. It made sense that Kitty had chosen this photo; it served both as a reminder than even when destroying the artwork she loved most in the world, she still hadn't lost Daniela.

Alec chose a photo of him, Kitty and me: I don't even remember it being taken. He had his arms around us both, all of us squinting against the sun. We looked deliriously happy: I missed that feeling. His other one was him and Soph in the same position as when I first met them; Sophie laying on the floor, Alec stood on the sofa. It was clear to anyone who knew them that they were in the middle of a heated Shakespeare contest. We rarely did them anymore - Sophie's constant silence made it difficult to carry them on; she was always the best at them.

Sophie only chose one photograph - it was all of us on stage after Alec's Present Laughter performance. It was imperfect; all of us sweating under the stage lights, Alec still in his tousled costume. It seemed fitting that she chose this one; Alec's role as Garry Essendine had become unfairly relevant - a depressed actor having a breakdown and struggling to love his craft.

I struggled to choose two photographs, simultaneously wanting to keep them all and also burn the lot of them. I managed to find some though, hidden by the fact that Ariel was curled up on top of a pile of them. One was the group photo we took during the Ancient Greek party, all of us draped in bed sheets and gold glitter. I'd forgotten how beautiful we all looked - the girls' hair threaded with ribbon, our eyes coated in glitter. It reminded me of Sophie's soft smile, the way she brushed her hand through my hair and whispered "Patroclus".

My final photo was a surprise to everyone, I think. It didn't have any of us in, but was instead just a photo of the Northam building. It had clearly been taken from the steps, the top of the roof just visible in shot. I know everyone else was questioning why I would ever choose a photo without anybody in, but this place meant just as much to me as the people in it.

The sad reality of the photos hit me that evening. Louis wasn't in any of them. Of course, we had other photos of him, we all took them too, but even with thousands of photos laid out in front of us, he'd never included himself. It made me even more determined to burn them all - if somebody found these photos it would paint a narrative of our life without Louis. I'd rather we all be forgotten than just him be left behind.

That thought was the only one which kept me going as we walked up the hill, each of us holding a box of photos. Dani made the fire, all of us stood around it.

"Should we say something?" Kitty asked softly, and all of us nodded. "I'll start then, I suppose. Lou, I'm sorry. I'm so sorry, and I miss you so much. You're the greatest person I know and you deserved to leave this place and go onto greater things more than anyone. I love you."

She wiped a tear away before putting the photos on the fire, wrapping her arms around herself. Dani squeezed her shoulder before stepping forward.

"Louis, looking through these photos, I realise just how much you saw, and how much you were here for. I wish you could have photographed the rest of my life, my friend, you should have outlasted us all."

Dani put her photos on, and we turned to Sophie. She was already crying, and merely closed her eyes, looked up, and smiled before placing her photos on the fire. It was more than enough.

"God, okay. Lou, I can't thank you enough for these photos. It hurts that you're not in them, but you're always in our memories and you always will be. You deserved a hell of a lot better, my friend."

I gave Alec a watery smile, feeling the pressure of everyone's eyes on me. It took me a minute to think of anything to say, before I realised that I could finally be honest. At the funeral, I had the eyes of an entire school on me, but out here everyone already knew the truth.

"Louis, I don't really need to say much. You already know it all, or at least I hope you do. God, I hope you know what you meant to me. You changed everything, and I wish I could have changed it all for you too. Shine bright, my love."

I placed the last of the photos on the fire, and stepped back. We stood there for the longest time, just watching the flames. In the distance I could hear the sound of various house parties, celebrating the end of term. We had a celebration, I suppose. It was just more of a celebration of life.

On the walk back down, I bit the bullet and pulled Alec slightly away from the group. I don't know why I chose him - maybe subconsciously I knew that Kitty could never keep the secret. I felt like I didn't really have a reason not to mention Archie to Alec, given that we were leaving tomorrow. I'd booked train tickets to Louis' parents, I'd phoned and asked if I could drop some of Louis' things at their house - I still needed to work on my excuse.

"Hey, um. Louis, before he died, was afraid of this guy following him. I don't know whether he was, but…" I trailed off, already knowing I'd lost Alec. He scoffed, rolling his eyes and taking my cigarette off me. He smiled sadly before squeezing my shoulder.

"Look, Seb. Don't get caught up in Louis' mania. He wasn't in the right state of mind at the end. Just forget about it and move on, yeah?"

It hurt to be dismissed in this way. It hurt more to know I had dismissed Louis in just the same way.

I didn't bring it up again. I'd travel to Louis' parents on my own, it seemed fitting.

When we headed back home, I made one last stop. I needed a moment in Louis' room before I left. I just stood there, looking around the room that I'd once been familiar with but hadn't properly been inside for months. I can't remember getting particularly upset, or even finding it difficult. I don't remember having any thoughts at all, really. I just stood there.

As I turned to leave, I noticed a piece of paper stuck to his wall, right opposite his bed. It looked as though he'd written it himself, I recognised his messy handwriting in the bold red marker.

"Any moment might be our last. Everything is more beautiful because we're doomed. We will never be here again."

It was the quote that had haunted me since his death. It was the quote I'd whispered to myself after we'd kissed, and the quote that had pounded through my head during the most stressful exam season. I'd never been able to piece together where I'd known that quote from, but now it seemed obvious. Of course it had been Louis. It always was.

I went to sleep that night knowing it was my last night at Northam, and yet I still found it easier to sleep. In fact, it was the first night I slept with the light off since the accident. I'd finally said goodbye to Louis properly, and that soothed me. I still didn't know how I would ever live life after Northam, but if I could survive it without Louis, I'd find a way.

CHAPTER SEVENTEEN

"Time's the king of men;

he's both their parent, and he is their grave,

and gives them what he will, not what they crave"

> *- Pericles*

Somehow, I managed to leave. I won't talk about the goodbyes from the next morning. We've had quite enough sadness. I managed to walk out the door and, having one final glance up at Northam, I walked away.

Returning home was disconcerting. It was as though life at home had paused whilst I was away, and all of a sudden it resumed, and I just had to catch up. I was a different person than when I left, but I was still expected to attend coffee mornings with my mother, still had to listen to my father talk about how history was a waste of time, still had to meet up with family I didn't know and friends I didn't like. Nobody here knew Louis, or Alec, or Kitty and Dani and Sophie. It should have felt refreshing, but it just felt lonely. I knew I would have to accept that, but it didn't come easily.

It felt as though I'd barely unpacked before I was on another train again, on my way to Louis' house. I'd thrown a few of his books and clothes into a box just before I'd left, hoping it would be enough to convince them to talk to me. I was nervous but excited; I remember being full of an odd sense of adrenaline. Finally, after what seemed to be forever, I was going to get some more answers.

Looking back, I realise I had no right to judge Louis for spiralling. I did the same thing. I didn't realise it at the time, but the mystery of Archie was practically the only thing I thought about. It became an incessant need to understand everything, get all the answers. Louis always wanted to understand the world, but I would have been satisfied with understanding him.

Louis' parents lived in an old countryhouse in the middle of a small village. It made me uneasy; I'd always grown up in a large city. There was always the comfort of anonymity in bigger cities. Here, it looked like everyone knew everybody. Their stories were intertwined. Maybe that explained why Louis had such a need to connect with people.

When I knocked on the door, I held my breath nervously. The last time I'd seen the Mitchells, the pain on their face had been shattering. I'd finally reached a point where I could function on a day to day basis without feeling like the earth was eating me up. Back when Louis had died, it felt like I was constantly toeing the edge of a cliff, the sinking feeling in my stomach a constant presence. It had taken a while to convince myself that I wasn't actually about to fall, but I'd finally reached that point. By the time I left Northam, I was still standing on the cliff, but I felt steady and secure.

As I walked into his house, I could feel the wind whistling past my ears and rocks crumbling beneath my feet.

The first thing I remembered was the absence of photos in the house. I'd always presumed Louis had inherited his love of photography from a parent, but other than official graduation photos and one or two wedding pictures, the walls were bare.

After a few pleasantries, I took a deep breath. I knew if I didn't say it straight away I would never say it. I owed it to Louis to get some of the answers he would never get.

"Mr Mitchell, Mrs Mitchell...I want to ask you a few questions about the last few weeks of Louis' life. I know it is upsetting but..." I remember swallowing some intense guilt. I had a habit, apparently, of dragging up other people's grief in order to soothe my own.

"Louis was convinced someone was following him. A man appeared in many of his photos, and despite me trying to convince him that it was a coincidence, it began to consume Louis. He went to visit the man just after Christmas, but found he had died." I paused, giving myself a chance to gage their reactions.

"Son, Louis was prone to neuroticism. He's always had these moments of obsession. Nobody would have been following him - like you said, it was a coincidence," his father told me, making me regret my dismissal of Louis even more.

"That's what I thought too...but I went to visit the man's widow. And whilst I was there, I noticed a photograph with you in it. Do you recognise him?"

I handed over the photo of Archie, and I instantly saw the ghosts of a dark secret flicker across their faces. At once, I knew I was going to receive an answer.

"Look, Sebastian...this is a long and complicated story-" his mother started, but I was shaking my head.

"Tell me everything. I need it- Louis was...I owe it to Louis to know the whole story. Please."

They exchanged a look which contained a multitude of thoughts, and then they told me.

I didn't get all the answers I needed. I'm afraid I can't tell you whether Archie was stalking him with harmful intentions, or whether his reasons were purer.

The story I was told was a classic one. A man, a woman, an unborn child. There was a break up, broken hearts all round. The woman moved to a small town in the country with the man she'd used to break the other man's heart. He moved to the village by his school, aware his child was growing up without him.

Maybe I'm confusing matters. Everything Archie's wife had told me was true: she'd started dating Archie after he broke up with his Northam girlfriend, and life went on. What she didn't know was that his Northam girlfriend had been pregnant, had ran off with one of their friends - Edward Mitchell - and raised their son with no contact from his birth father.

As I sat at the kitchen table that day, trying to wrap my head around it all, I had one overwhelming thought - had Louis survived, which father would he have taken after? Edward: successful, loving father, in a job he loved? Or Archie: dissatisfied, failed artist, lost. He clearly thought the latter, not that he ever knew his parentage. I disagreed, and still do. Louis shone too brightly for him to ever be dimmed in that way. It still didn't explain whether Archie meant him harm - was he out for revenge, resenting the son he never got to know? Did he hate Louis for being everything he'd wanted in life? Or did he want to have a relationship with Louis - maybe he merely wanted to know his son. This whole story is based on one word: maybe.

Maybe if the Mitchells had told Louis about Archie, he'd have stopped the spiral before it even began. Maybe if Archie had reached out properly, he wouldn't have driven Louis to his death. Maybe if Louis had noticed the picture of his parents in Archie's house, he would have thought to question his parents, and gotten the answers he so clearly needed.

Maybe if I'd noticed the closed door.

On the train back home, I tried to sift through my emotions. I'd found that was the easiest way to deal with them - imagine them as physical objects that simply needed dealing with. For the first time since his death, the guilt seemed manageable. It was ever present - it still is - but I remember feeling satisfied that I had, at least, gotten some answers. It felt almost as if I could survive going back to my parents and dealing with the suffocating reality of normalcy.

I didn't have all the answers, but I'd closed the book on this particular story.

CHAPTER EIGHTEEN

"Purpose is but the slave to memory,

Of violent birth, but poor validity;

Which now, like fruit unripe, sticks on the tree;

But fall, unshaken, when they mellow be.

Most necessary 'tis that we forget

To pay ourselves what to ourselves is debt"

- *Hamlet*

We were a month into the holiday when a letter arrived for me. It confused me at first - the envelope was one of the fancy, stiff ones, and my name was written in italic calligraphy.

I grinned when I first opened it. It was very clearly Kitty's attempt to make us all think she was inviting us to a sophisticated attempt. She was reaching the end of her extension for her art project, and the invite was for her final unveiling. There was never any doubt, of course, that I would attend, even if it seemed to be tempting fate to make myself say goodbye to the place twice.

That was how I found myself back on a train, staring up at the familiar station once again.

The exhibition wasn't being held in Northam, and I thanked my lucky stars for that. I walked through campus and once again was struck with the realisation that life here had continued without us too. I'd never spent much time in the exhibition hall, and yet when I walked in I was hit with familiarity.

I was also hit with Kitty, running and flinging her arms around me. I laughed out loud, wrapping my arms around her too.

"KitKat, let the boy breathe!" Dani cried, giving me another hug. I hugged them both back, getting another one from Alec. Sophie approached me shyly, biting her lip. As I wrapped my arms around her I saw Teddy behind her, and I raised an eyebrow at Sophie. She blushed, and I grinned. I wanted nothing more than for her to be happy. I hadn't realised she'd even kept in touch with him after the ball, but I was glad she did.

"So, Kitty. Ready to finally graduate?" I teased, and her expression immediately turned nervous. The painting was up on the stage, covered by a green velvet cloth. There was a podium up there too, and I eagerly awaited the unveiling.

"This better be good, Miss 'I couldn't make our anniversary dinner because I was holed up in our studio'", Dani teased, trying to make Kitty smile again.

"Oh, I'm sorry. Didn't realise that the burned mess you presented me with counted as dinner," Kitty replied, the kiss she pressed against Dani's cheek undercutting any tension her words could have held.

As I watched the whole group stand in a circle and tease each other, I could feel the tension I didn't realise I was holding in my stomach release. I'd been so worried that we'd return and the dynamic would be off, that time away would put too much pressure on us all and suddenly we wouldn't fit together again. But it truly seemed like nothing had changed. I briefly considered telling someone - anyone - about what I had unearthed at the Mitchells, but ultimately I knew I never would. They didn't need to know. That conclusion was only needed for people who had been on this whole journey, and that wasn't them. They didn't need to know about Louis' turmoil, but instead they should remember him as they already did.

Eventually the Head of Art walked in and we all took our seats. Kitty was sat next to me, her legs jittering as she was introduced.

"So without further ado, I'm pleased to invite Katherine Winters to come and speak us through her final piece."

Kitty stood at the podium, locked eyes with us all and took a deep breath.

"Hi guys. Thank you all for coming here today. I'd briefly considered skipping this myself, to be honest, but it felt wrong to not invite you all. I think it'll probably be easier to just show you the painting and then explain it. So let me just say this: the painting I'm about to show you is the most important one of my career so far, and it means the world to me. I hope it means the same to you."

She took a deep breath, closed her eyes, nodded, and pulled the cloth away.

Louis was staring back at us.

It was, in a word, magical. The likeness was incredible - his eyes the perfect colour, his curls falling just as though he was in the room with us. It made my heart ache. But the most exceptional part was his expression. It felt exactly like he was staring at me, a small, soft smile on his face. She'd perfectly caught the reflection in his glasses, each freckle perfect. It was clear she'd used one of the photos from the Ancient Greek party, because gold was littered across his cheekbones, gold leaves threaded through his hair. I would never understand how she made the paint sparkle like that, but I would forever be in awe of it.

Kitty glanced back at us with tears in her eyes, no doubt taking in our open mouthed shock. She smiled before clearing her throat, walking back towards the podium.

"I don't want this to be another eulogy for Louis, so I'll try and keep it brief. If I could have painted each and every one of you, I would. The brief for the piece was the concept of hope, and from then on I knew I would paint Louis. It might seem weird - he'd so clearly lost hope by the time he died, so how could I say he represented hope? I don't really have an answer for you, but honestly, it's just a word I've always associated with him. He gave me hope when he was alive, and I like to think he still brings me hope now. This artwork was my second chance, a second chance that I wish he'd been awarded. Thank you all for coming here today, and thank you for getting me through the last year."

We all applauded Kitty until the professor held up her hand for quiet.

"I'd just like to add one extra announcement. As I'm sure you know, Louis' family gave us a generous donation to upgrade the photography studio on campus. We, the school administration, would like Kitty's artwork to hang in the entrance to the newly named Louis Mitchell Photography Studio."

None of us really reacted until she'd left the room, leaving us sitting there with silent tears rolling down our face. Kitty was sobbing, both through relief, pride and grief. I knew how she felt. It felt like my brain couldn't really decide which emotion to go with, so they simply all mixed together, making me a little dizzy.

"Kitty, it's stunning. It really is. We're so proud of you," Alec said finally, accepting her tearful hug. Nobody said much after that; there wasn't much to say.

When we finally began to think about leaving, Sophie and Teddy approached me. Teddy looked a little awkward, and I was reminded once again that we barely knew each other. Soph hadn't kept his a secret, as such, but she'd certainly made no attempt to integrate him into Northam. It made sense, I suppose. Who would want to bring anyone into that chaos?

"Hi, Seb, um...Sophie wanted to give you this. She found it in Louis' room, that day before we all left. It's addressed to you."

I stared at them both as Soph handed me a letter, gave me one of her trademark soft smiles, and walked away. If I hadn't been so preoccupied by the letter in my hand, it might have broken my heart to see her walk away again. I suppose shock overpowered sadness, once again.

I didn't read the letter there. It wasn't the place, or time. Thinking about Louis was to be done in private, and truthfully, I was scared of what it would contain. So I simply pocketed it. Another time, another day. I'd waited this long to hear from him again, I could wait a little longer.

It brought me great comfort to know the photography studio was named after Louis. I'd been so scared that he would be forgotten, left behind by the passage of time, but this made it impossible. He would forever be known for the thing he loved the most; his art. As long as there were people like him to keep the love of art alive - and people like Kitty to keep his legacy alive, there would always be room for artists.

EPILOGUE

"My Tongue is Weary; when My Legs Are Too, I Will Bid You Goodnight."

- *Henry IV*

You might not want to hear this, but I don't have all the answers. Still to this day, I wish that I did, but I don't.

I still don't know what went wrong.

If you're hoping for a satisfying ending where we unearth a mystery and solve all of our problems, this is the wrong story. Sometimes life just doesn't have answers, and this is proof. I wish I did have the answers - I wish I could tell you why Archie was in those photos. Why was he following Louis? Did he actually pose the threat Louis thought he did, or did he simply want to know his son? Did Louis even know there was a connection, or was he simply a sad, lonely boy who was forced into a downward spiral he just couldn't escape from. As much as I hate to admit it, I think it's the latter. I say I hate to admit it, because maybe then I could have done something to help. I might not have been able to stop a stalker, but I should have been able to help my own friend. But again, sometimes life just doesn't work like that.

I can offer you somewhat of a conclusion on everyone else, at least. Maybe conclusion is the wrong word. Their stories aren't over, and hopefully they won't be for a long time.

Kitty and Daniela are still hopelessly in love. I saw them last year, at a celebration for the anniversary of Kitty's sobriety. It wasn't a straight line - she has not been sober since that first day at the sink, pouring the bottles down the drain. She caused hurt and pain to everyone who loved her, no more so than Dani. But ultimately, she worked on it, she got better, and we adore her for it. She genuinely cares about other people, and we give it back two-fold. Like I always said: she lived to put beauty into the world, and in the form of Dani, it gave it back to her.

Alec is, unsurprisingly, the most successful of us all. I went to every bad local play he put on until I finally saw him in something worthy of his talents. The first time I saw his name in the newspaper, I thought I might cry with pride. It referred to him by his full name, and barely a day later I received a phone call from Kitty, laughing hysterically. Some things never changed.

To this day I've never heard Sophie speak again, but I've been assured that's soon to change. She's spoken to Kitty now and then, and I've been assured she's happy. I have my doubts - Sophie never quite let on just how she was feeling - but I trust that she's doing well. The last thing I heard from her was an invite to her and Teddy's wedding. I can't wait to hear her say her vows.

I haven't yet found someone to replace Louis. Maybe one day, I'll stop thinking of it as Louis' position. I've dated here and there, boyfriends and girlfriends have come and gone, but none have mattered quite as much as him. I have hope though. One day, maybe. It doesn't matter either way though. Maybe I'm not made to have great, magical love stories. Maybe I'm just meant to document them.

Talking of great magical love stories, I suppose I better tell you about the letter. I don't have anything to add to it, so I'll just copy it out. It would be wrong to change his words anyway: he created, I documented. He was the one who used his words, I was the one who listened to them. I won't add anything, so read it as I did. But first - a note from Sophie.

"Seb,

I found this in his desk. I wanted to wait until we'd left Northam to give it to you, because I don't know what your reaction would be, and I can't see you break down. If you need me though, I'm always here. I haven't read it, it's for your eyes only.

He really loved you, Seb. We all did. Never doubt how special you were to us.

Love always, Soph"

...

"Sebastian,

I know you probably hate me. I deserve it, I'm sure. Even I'm not confident I'm making the right choice, maybe this will never be needed. But in case it is:

This is not your fault. I don't know whether you have told the others about the man in the photos, either way it doesn't matter. I only told you because I felt like you were the only one who ever needed to know. For me, there was never any other.

Seb, you spend your life trying to be worthy of others. Stop it. Please. You don't need to try and be worthy, you always have been. You're a much better person than you give yourself credit for.

I don't know how much more I can say. I'm sorry for what I will inevitably put you through.

One last quote, to leave you with. You said it to me last night, and it really sums you up, I think.

"There's something awfully sad about happiness, isn't there?"

That might be the last thing you ever say to me, and it's kind of perfect don't you think? Seb, I know you think about sadness a lot, but please stop. Try and find a bit of happiness too? For me.

One last thing - did you ever understand the reason behind Achilles and Patroclus? I hope you did.

You're better than you know. You always have been.

All my love,

Louis."

*

Happiness is awfully sad, but it's awfully happy too.

Focus on that.

EXEUNT

28348532R00088

I FORGOT!

LEARNING ABOUT FOLLOWING INSTRUCTIONS

Katherine Eason

FOX EYE
PUBLISHING

Hakeem **DIDN'T** always **FOLLOW INSTRUCTIONS**. When Hakeem didn't follow instructions, he got into a muddle.

2

Sometimes, Hakeem **FORGOT** the instructions. Sometimes, he **DIDN'T LISTEN**. Sometimes, he thought it **DIDN'T MATTER**.

On Monday, it was football club. Mum told Hakeem to put his football boots in his bag.

But Hakeem saw his favourite football top in the wardrobe. He put it in his bag. He **FORGOT** about his boots.

After school, Hakeem got changed for football practice. But there were no football boots in the bag. Hakeem had **FORGOTTEN** them!

Without his boots, Hakeem
COULDN'T JOIN IN.

On Tuesday, Mr Satchel gave the class a letter about a museum trip. He said to give the letter to their parents.

But Hakeem was talking with his friend. He missed the instruction because he **WASN'T LISTENING.**

The next day, Mr Satchel said Hakeem couldn't go on the museum trip, because Hakeem hadn't given his parents the letter.

10

Again, Hakeem COULDN'T JOIN IN.

On Friday, Miss Splash took the class swimming. She told them not to run by the pool. But Hakeem didn't follow her instructions. He thought it **DIDN'T MATTER**.

12

Hakeem ran around the pool. He slipped and fell. He hurt his elbow.

13

After school, Hakeem told Mum about his day. It had not been good! Mum gave Hakeem a cuddle. Then she said that following instructions was important. They kept you **SAFE**. They helped you to **JOIN IN**, too. She asked Hakeem how his day might have been if he had **LISTENED** to the instructions.

Hakeem thought about it. His day would have been **A LOT BETTER**. Perhaps following instructions was important after all.

The next week, Hakeem listened carefully in class. He wrote things in his homework diary. He tried hard to follow instructions.

Hakeem joined in with all the activities. He **FELT HAPPY**. Hakeem had learnt to **FOLLOW INSTRUCTIONS!**

Words and Behaviour

Hakeem didn't follow instructions in this story and that caused a lot of problems.

There are a lot of words to do with following instructions in this book. Can you remember all of them?

INSTRUCTIONS

JOIN IN

SAFE

19

Let's talk about feelings and manners

This series helps children to understand difficult emotions and behaviours and how to manage them. The characters in the series have been created to show emotions and behaviours that are often seen in young children, and which can be difficult to manage.

I Forgot!

The story in this book examines the reasons for following instructions. It looks at why following instructions is important and how it helps people to join in and keep safe.

How to use this book

You can read this book with one child or a group of children. The book can be used to begin a discussion around complex behaviour such as following instructions.

The book is also a reading aid, with enlarged and repeated words to help children to develop their reading skills.

How to read the story

Before beginning the story, ensure that the children you are reading to are relaxed and focused.

Take time to look at the enlarged words and the illustrations, and discuss what this book might be about before reading the story.

New words can be tricky for young children to approach. Sounding them out first, slowly and repeatedly, can help children to learn the words and become familiar with them.

How to discuss the story

When you have finished reading the story, use these questions and discussion points to examine the theme of the story with children and explore the emotions and behaviour within it:

- What do you think the story was about?
- Have you been in a situation in which you didn't follow instructions? What was that situation?
- Do you think following instructions doesn't matter? Why?
- Do you think following instructions is important? Why?
- What could go wrong if you don't follow instructions?

Titles in the series

   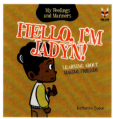 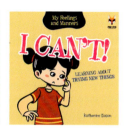

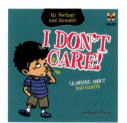    

  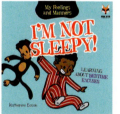 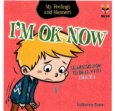 

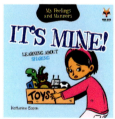    

First published in 2023 by Fox Eye Publishing
Unit 31, Vulcan House Business Centre,
Vulcan Road, Leicester, LE5 3EF
www.foxeyepublishing.com

Author: Katherine Eason
Art director: Paul Phillips
Cover designer: Emma Bailey
Editor: Jenny Rush

All illustrations by Novel

ISBN 978-1-80445-164-9

Printed in China